Missing Persons
The First Buddy Steel Thriller

"*Missing Persons* is a cracking series debut, and Buddy Steel is a protagonist bound to have a long shelf life."

—Reed Farrel Coleman, *New York Times*
bestselling author of *What You Break*

"Fans of Parker's work will appreciate Buddy, another irreverent, complex lawman."

—*Library Journal*

"Michael Brandman's follow-up to the three Jesse Stone novels he adeptly penned for the late Robert B. Parker gives us the cool and iconic Buddy Steel. A former point guard turned cop, Steel damn sure owns the ground he walks on. All capable 6'3" and 170 pounds of him, Buddy's that guy that you want to ride with when s..t hits the fan. With plenty of thrilling moments and turns you don't see coming, what a great ride Brandman takes us on in *Missing Persons*. Trust me, you won't be disappointed. Buckle up."

—Robert Knott, *New York Times* bestselling
author of the Hitch and Cole Series

RISK
FACTOR

Also by Michael Brandman

The Buddy Steel Thrillers
Missing Persons
One on One
Wild Card

The Jesse Stone Novels
Robert B. Parker's Fool Me Twice
Robert B. Parker's Killing the Blues
Robert B. Parker's Damned If You Do

RISK FACTOR

A BUDDY STEEL THRILLER

MICHAEL BRANDMAN

Poisoned Pen
PRESS

Published by Poisoned Pen Press, an imprint of Sourcebooks
P.O. Box 4410, Naperville, Illinois 60567-4410
(630) 961-3900
sourcebooks.com

Library of Congress Cataloging-in-Publication Data

Names: Brandman, Michael, author.
Title: Risk factor / Michael Brandman.
Description: Naperville : Poisoned Pen Press, [2021] | Series: A Buddy
   Steel thriller
Identifiers: LCCN 2019049438 | (hardcover)
Subjects: GSAFD: Mystery fiction.
Classification: LCC PS3602.R356 R54 2021 | DDC 813/.6--dc23
LC record available at https://lccn.loc.gov/2019049438

Printed and bound in the United States of America.
SB 10 9 8 7 6 5 4 3 2 1

For Joanna…

The brightest star in the galaxy…

…with my undying love

risk factor:

a heightened possibility of danger

ONE

The first place they hit was my father's house.

The Sheriff and my stepmother, Regina Goodnow, the mayor of Freedom Township, discovered the break-in when they returned from a Palm Springs weekend.

The thieves had grabbed whatever small valuables were lying around, including some of Regina's cherished jewelry and a pair of antique watches. They swept the bathroom clean of prescription medications. They cracked the master bedroom's hidden wall safe and ransacked it.

The police surmised it was the work of burglars who had recently pillaged a number of upscale homes in the Santa Barbara area.

They appeared to have had knowledge of the layout of the house. They were expert in disarming the security alarm system. None of the neighbors had seen nor heard anything out of the ordinary.

At the time, I was on a sabbatical. Time spent away from the San Remo Sheriff's Department, where I had been working alongside my father as his deputy.

No sooner had the old man been elected to a third term as County Sheriff than he was diagnosed with ALS, Amyotrophic Lateral Sclerosis, aka Lou Gehrig's disease.

When he continued to respond positively to a new pharmaceutical that promised to slow the progress of the disease, everyone breathed a sigh of relief.

I took it as my cue to grab some much-needed downtime in which to rest, reinvigorate, reevaluate, and pay heed to my own psychological well-being.

I am currently in Deer Valley, Utah, in a rustic cabin that belongs to Jordyn Yates, who is not only my attorney, but also a woman with whom I'm sharing a newly rejuvenated romance.

By way of introduction, my name is Buddy Steel. Actually it's Burton Steel Jr. I'm a thirty-three-year-old law enforcement professional, currently experiencing what might be termed a midlife meltdown.

Footloose, seeking answers to questions I've yet to even formulate, I'd spent the last several weeks beachcombing the Mexican coastline from Cancun to the Riviera Maya.

Now, in search of a breath of non-salty air, I am enjoying the rugged peaks and canyons of the Wasatch Mountain range, whose sharp ridgelines stand watch over verdant fields and Alpine lakes that were originally formed by ancient, Pleistocene-era glaciers.

Because I had been off the grid for a while, the ringing of my cell phone startled me.

"Buddy," I answered.

"Is that you?" Captain Marsha Russo of the San Remo County Sheriff's office responded.

"Marsha?"

"Buddy?"

"Yes."

"It's really you."

"Was there a reason for this call, Marsha?"

"Are you sitting down?"

"What is it?"

"Your family manse was hit last night."

"Meaning?"

"Burglary. High-end professional job. Upset the old man terribly."

"Meaning?"

"He wants you."

"In what way?"

"In the '*I Need Buddy To Come Home*' way. '*Immediately.*'"

"Shit."

"I knew you'd say that."

"What were his exact words?"

"'*Locate him and get his ass back here.*'"

"That's what he said?"

"More than once. And I omitted the profanities."

"Tell him you can't find me."

"No."

"What, no? Just tell him I didn't answer my phone."

"May I say something in confidence, Buddy?"

"What?"

"You're fucked. How soon can you be here?"

TWO

It took more than half a day to make the drive, and I pulled the Wrangler into the garage of my condo in Freedom sometime after two a.m. I showed up at the office at ten.

I was in the throes of determining just how depressed I was when Marsha stepped into my office and dropped down in one of the two visitor's chairs. "You don't look any different."

I gave her my best dead-eyed stare. "Where is he?"

"It's nice to have you back, Buddy."

"Let's not get ahead of ourselves here, okay? Nobody said I was back."

She flashed me a crooked grin. "He's at the house. With Johnny Kennerly. It hit him hard."

"The break-in?"

"And the loss of his stuff."

"The safe?"

"Lots of valuable stuff in such a small safe."

"Such as?"

"Wills. Deeds. Titles. Plus a bundle of cash."

"Replaceable?"

"That's an insurance company question. But the vulnerability proved difficult for them."

"Them being himself and Her Honor?"

"You're so perceptive, Buddy."

"You were saying…"

"We're seeing a bunch of similar home invasions. Most recently in Santa Barbara County. Now here. All targeting the rich and famous."

"He knows I'm in town?"

"He can hardly contain himself."

"Shit."

"How did I know you'd come to that realization?"

My father and the mayor live in one of the more upscale neighborhoods of Freedom, the two of them puttering around the creaky old mansion in which I grew up.

As I climbed the steps to the front porch, my thoughts were of my late mother. I knew when I stepped inside I'd be confronted with the reality that everything which reflected her personal tastes and interests had either been overhauled or replaced by my stepmother.

But in that brief instant, after ringing the bell and waiting for the door to open, I fantasized I would be entering the cherished dwelling of my youth. Exactly as it had been.

"Buddy," Regina pronounced as she enveloped me in a bear hug.

She wore a modest blue suit, a gray silk T-shirt, and a look of grave concern.

She gave me the once-over. "You don't look any more rested or relaxed for all your highfalutin gallivanting."

"Nice to see you, too, Regina."

She closed the door behind us. "He's with Johnny."

She led me to the kitchen, which had come to serve as her in-house operations center. "Can I get you anything?" she asked as she pointed me to a seat at the large, round, polished-oak table that dominated the room.

"I'm good. Thanks."

She sat across from me, in front of a pile of papers and a half-empty coffee mug. "This has upset him terribly."

"Tell me."

"He's always considered the house inviolate. His castle, so to speak. His refuge. The break-in and thefts shattered that image. He hasn't been the same since we discovered it."

At that moment my father stormed into the kitchen, followed by his longtime protégé and current deputy, Johnny Kennerly, a large man of color who was totally devoted to him.

"I told you I heard voices," he tossed over his shoulder to Johnny.

He briefly embraced me, then gave me the once-over. "You need a haircut."

I exchanged smiles with Johnny.

"Good time?" he inquired.

"Better than a good time."

"You look great."

"I feel great."

My father sneered. "How much longer will this bromance hooyah go on?"

"Nothing changes," I said to Johnny.

"Tell me about it. While you were away finding yourself, I was here. With him."

"Grim?"

"Worse."

"This is like a fucking episode of *The Real Housewives of New Jersey*," my father snarled to Regina.

"Burton, please…" she replied.

THREE

"Turns out the LAPD was tracking residential break-ins not only in Los Angeles, but as far north as Santa Barbara, too," Johnny told me. "The burglary at your house echoed the tactics of those invasions.

"The crime unit's assessment is that these break-ins are the work of professionals who appear to have now found greener pastures in our neck of the woods."

We were seated alone on the mansion's back porch, my father and stepmother having busied themselves with their respective activities. The heavy oceanic atmosphere, pungent with the promise of rain, was a far cry from the crisp mountain air I had just left.

"What is it you're not telling me?"

"He's a mess," Johnny said. "Not that he'll show it to you. The meds are still working, if that's what you're thinking. It's his spirit that's been crushed."

"Because?"

"Psychologically speaking, I believe he's equating the home invasion with his physical vulnerability. For the first time I think he's coming to grips with his mortality."

"And?"

"It's cost him."

"Cost him how?"

"Although he won't admit it, I think he's thrown in the towel. All he's trying to do is find a way out."

"Of life?"

"Of the job. That's why he was so insistent you get back here."

"To what end?"

"He told me you'd be returning to your old position."

"He told you what?"

"You heard me. Are you?"

"Returning to the job?"

Johnny nodded.

I shrugged. "It never occurred to me."

FOUR

The new break-in was at the home of Chet Forster, the Los Angeles Clippers' star forward.

Forster, his wife, and their two young children were on the island of Antigua, in a rented beachfront villa, relaxing following a grueling basketball season.

By the time the home security service arrived at Forster's home in the Freedom foothills, the burglars were gone, having taken with them several mementos of his illustrious career... rings, belts, and medals.

They had also grabbed jewelry, a silver service, and the contents of a wall safe that contained a cache of securities and cash. In all, they made off with items worth close to a quarter of a million dollars.

It was Johnny Kennerly who responded to the home security service's call. And although my status was in limbo, he summoned me and, as in times past, we rode together to the crime scene.

"You had dinner with them?" Johnny asked.

"Yes."

"So? How does the Sheriff seem to you?"

"You were right."

"Meaning?"

"He's tired. His stamina seems low. He's distracted and even worse, indifferent."

"Did you sort out your feelings about any of this crap during your sabbatical?"

"Not exactly."

"Well, I sure hope you're prepared to decide."

"Decide what?"

"What happens in chapter two of the life story of Burton Steel Jr."

———

I trailed Johnny as he made his way through each of the many rooms of the Forster estate, stopping to study more carefully the burglars' entrance point—the kitchen door, beside which the main security terminal was affixed.

"A conundrum," he muttered.

"How so?"

He looked at me blank-eyed, still deep in thought. "Two conundrums, actually."

"Do you want to share them?"

"How did they know where the wall safe was located? And how did they disable the alarm system? Events similar to the earlier crimes."

He summoned the alarm system techie who had been assigned to assist during Johnny's investigation. He pointed the techie to the wall-mounted terminal and asked, "Why didn't the break-in activate the alarm?"

A weathered man in his middle years, the techie removed the terminal's cover and stood studying it for a while. He then programmed a series of protocols into the system which proved inconclusive. "Good question."

"Do you see any irregularities?"

"None I can identify. Everything seems to be in order."

"Why didn't it activate?"

"I don't really know."

"Could they have temporarily disabled it?"

"It would seem so, but I can't see how."

"Can the system be controlled from a remote location?"

"Yes."

"Where?"

"From the main facility."

"From the security company's main facility?"

"In Pacoima."

"In Southern California Pacoima?"

"Yes."

"Was it deactivated by someone in Pacoima?"

"Not to my knowledge."

"Did you inquire as to whether or not it was?"

"Do I look like a total idiot to you?"

Johnny glared at him. "I'm not trying to demean you, sir. But did you ask if anyone based in Pacoima disabled the Forster alarm system?"

"Of course I did."

"And?"

"None of the operators on duty at the time of the burglary claimed to have done so."

"But could they have?"

"I suppose they could have, but it's not likely."

"Because?"

"There were three operators on duty at the time of the break-in. One of them would surely have noticed if either of the other two had disabled the system."

"And from that you infer?"

"I don't infer shit. The system was disabled by the perpetrators. I haven't a clue as to how."

FIVE

After completing the investigation, Johnny and I sat for a while on a bench at the northern end of Freedom Park, located on a verdant bluff overlooking the Pacific.

"What are you thinking?" I asked him.

"Nothing concrete."

"Meaning?"

"If this crime is similar to the modus operandi of the other break-ins, there's something missing in our assessment of them."

"Meaning?"

"I don't know, Buddy. There's something inexplicable about it."

"Like what?"

"Something more insidious than just break-ins and thefts. These bozos have too much information."

"Such as?"

"They're knowledgeable about the homes they invade. Based

in part on publicly available information. Not only regarding the identities of the victims, but as to their comings and goings as well. Celebrities are obvious targets because of how public their lives are.

"Take this basketball player. This Forster guy. They were likely hip to his travel plans because he revealed them on Twitter. If you know what you're looking for, it's not hard to find it."

"All this is pretty common knowledge, John."

"I'm not saying anything other than that. But there's another ingredient. Like with the previous robberies. It's what baffled the security system techie. And me, too, for that matter."

"And that is?"

"How did they know so much about the layout of each place? And how did they disable the alarm systems?"

"Good questions."

"With no good answers."

I suggested to Johnny that he scour the venues where the looted property might be listed for sale and that he explore whether inquiries had been made to the Realty Property offices in Santa Barbara County and in Santa Rosa by any so-called Realtors or developers regarding access to blueprints and building plans they might have on file.

Then I went to see my father.

He was on his favorite chair, in his cherished spot on the back porch. I dropped into the love seat across from him.

"Gin?" he inquired.

"With lemonade."

"Yuck. I can't for the life of me figure out why you like that drink."

"Yours is not to reason why."

"I know. I know."

He fixed it and placed it in front of me. I raised my glass to him. "To life."

He raised his glass of Johnnie Walker Black. "What's left of it."

We drank.

A baby wren fluttered onto the porch, looked at each of us, then fled. The old man sighed deeply. "I'm tired, Buddy."

"So take a few days off. Get some rest."

"It's not that kind of tired."

"Meaning?"

"I'm irrelevant."

"What are you getting at?"

"I've been wrestling with who and what I am, and I've come to realize I'm no more than a clueless old white man. Still observing the tenets of the twentieth century and totally baffled by what's taking place today.

"I barely understand you and your Generation X. I have no comprehension whatsoever of these so-called millennials. They're nothing like us. They don't think like us. And although I hold some sway by virtue of my job, to them, I'm invisible. Irrelevant."

"Don't be so hard on yourself, Dad."

"Hard on myself? Every day I wake up puzzled. I try to convince myself I know what I'm doing. And you know what? So does every other member of our so-called Greatest Generation. Somebody needs to stick a fork in all of us because we're done."

He took another chug of Johnnie Black. "I'm one of the lucky ones, Buddy. I've been thrown a lifeline. This new medication has given me some time. And what I now know is that it's time I don't want to spend in a fruitless quest trying to understand what in the hell is going on around me. I'm planning to resign."

"What?"

"I'm going to step down. Name a successor. A temporary appointment until an election can be held."

"That's some bombshell."

"And it's not all. I want you back as my chief deputy. And I want to stand behind your candidacy for the job."

"You mean you want me to succeed you permanently?"

"Yes."

"Why would I do that?"

"It's your most logical career move."

"Do I have any say in the matter?"

He stared at me and said nothing.

"I came back because I felt I could help you weather this home invasion meshugas. But to be totally clear, that's the only reason I'm here. Not to pick up where I left off. And certainly not to succeed you."

"We'll see."

"We've already seen. I'm not your deputy. And I'm most assuredly not a candidate. If you're looking for a successor, Johnny's your man."

"We'll see."

SIX

For want of something to do, and following a hunch, I got in my Wrangler and headed north to the Cal Poly campus.

California Polytechnic State University is located in San Luis Obispo, often referred to as "one of the happiest cities in the United States."

Founded in 1771 by the Spanish Franciscan, Junipero Serra, it's also one of California's oldest communities.

I was trying to come to grips with it being such a happy place versus the nature of one of its most notable citizens, Professor Lothar Diggins.

Diggins is the epitome of the cranky scientist: rumpled, grim-faced, dour, and short-tempered. Yet, he was Cal Poly's shining star, a world-renowned educator whose classes were booked years in advance.

He had been my high school science teacher, a job he briefly held while he was gathering credentials for a position in even higher education.

Clearly, I was a problem student, possessing little or no interest whatsoever in what he taught.

But for some unknown reason, he took a shine to me and as such, made me his *project*. He drove me mercilessly until I began to exhibit at least a meager understanding of his teachings. When I managed a B+, he took it as one of his major achievements. He bragged about me at every turn.

Our proximity tended to break down any barriers that might have existed between us and, try as I might not to, I found myself enjoying his company. He wasn't a whole lot older than me, and his juvenile behavior was a great equalizer.

We hung out together and were frequently asked to leave any number of museums and theaters and restaurants, the result of our uncontrollable laughter at things only we found funny.

His mien changed noticeably when he spotted me waiting for him in front of Science Hall.

The first thing he did was to hurriedly hide behind a nearby tree, pretending I couldn't see him. Nor he me. It was all downhill from there.

When the shenanigans finally subsided, we embraced and made tracks for the teacher's union, a self-service cafeteria/lounge. Over coffee and red velvet cupcakes, we caught each other up on our various career and life trajectories.

"So," he said, "what is it you want to know, Buddy?"

"How hot and cold might affect wiring."

"Really?"

"Yes."

"That isn't a question I'd ever in a million years expect from you."

"Who cares?"

He laughed. "Which do you want, hot or cold?"

"Cold."

"Cold as in cold or freezing cold?"

"Freezing cold."

"Wiring as in internal or external wiring?"

"Both."

"To what end?"

"Interruption of service."

"To a box or an edifice?"

"Box."

"A solid box or a control box?"

"Control."

"Permanent or temporary?"

"Temporary."

"Long temporary or short temporary?"

"Short."

"What freezing agent?"

"Unknown."

"Cream or spray?"

"I'd guess spray."

"So what you're asking is if one were to spray a freezing agent on wiring that exists both within and outside of some kind of electronic control box, would the service to that box be impeded in any way?"

"Something like that. Yes."

"Yes."

"Yes, what?"

"Yes it would impede service."

"How?"

"That's a variable depending on the quality and the quantity of the freezing agent."

"Unknown."

"Then, simply put, yes. Someone with the appropriate knowledge and proper skill can disable a control box by reducing its operational temperature to below freezing."

"I knew I'd come to the right place."

"You're welcome. You'll be receiving my bill shortly."

SEVEN

Aimless and untethered, I nonetheless checked in with Marsha Russo and learned that Johnny Kennerly was in the office. I asked her to let him know I was on my way to see him.

I shared an unusual connection with Johnny that, in an odd way, bound us. He had initially met my father when, during his junior year at Roosevelt High in North Freedom, his class visited the Sheriff's office.

After touring the station, and listening to my father's lecture on police work as a desirable career, Johnny started hanging around, offering to do odd jobs, repeatedly expressing his interest in law enforcement.

Impressed by his zeal, the Sheriff offered him a summer internship and he jumped at it. They became close. My father saw Johnny as the son he wished I was. A son who sought his counsel and was influenced by his wisdom.

Impressed that Johnny was a high school honors student, the Sheriff met and came to admire his hardworking, single-parent mother. As a result, he anonymously paid Johnny's college tuition out of his own pocket and upon his graduation, offered him a full-time job.

By the time he was diagnosed with ALS and I had agreed to join the department as my father's deputy, Johnny had also achieved deputy status.

Innately understanding the complicated nature of my relationship with the Sheriff, Johnny went out of his way to support me. He also made it his business to be a friend to my father as well.

Yet, although we both did our best to conceal it, there existed an unspoken tension between us. He was the favorite probationer. I was the prodigal son.

I knew he breathed a sigh of relief when I left the department for my sabbatical. Neither of us expected me to return. But now that I'm back, although not in any official capacity, my uncertainty has given birth to his. Because, in an odd way, we're brothers.

I sat down across from him.

"What brings you to Valhalla?" he jibed.

"Yes, the wiring both inside and outside of a security control box can cause disruption to the service if frozen."

"No shit."

"That answers one question. What about any Real Property inquiries?"

"There's a two-pronged answer."

"Prong one?"

"Inquiries were indeed made in Santa Barbara. Seems someone who had announced herself as a real estate broker, acting on behalf of a wealthy client, had been given access to the blueprints and floor plans of at least four houses."

"And?"

"There may have been others, but they hadn't been recorded."

"And the four houses?"

"All of them victims of home invasions. All of them suffering significant losses."

"And the broker?"

"Nonexistent. Phony address. Phony person."

"Prong two?"

"You mean San Remo County?"

"If that's the second prong."

"It is."

"And?"

"Nada."

"Nothing? No inquiries?"

"Correct."

I took in this information and sat quietly for a while.

"What?" Johnny asked.

"Odd."

"What odd?"

"If it's the same team, why the change in protocols? Why Santa Barbara and not San Remo?"

"Another good question."

"Without a good answer."

"What do you think?"

"Further investigation required."

"Meaning you're stepping into it?"

"I'm not going that far, John. But it's intriguing."

We shared an uncomfortable silence, both of us unaware of the shit that was about to hit the proverbial fan.

EIGHT

Sleep was elusive, and after what seemed like hours of tossing and turning, I finally drifted off only to be jarred awake by my cell phone.

When I answered, I noticed it was 3:30 a.m. "This better be good," I said.

"It's pretty bad," Deputy Sheriff Dave Balding whipped back.

"Tell me."

"We've got a hostage situation."

"Go on."

"It's my night in the barrel and nothing out of the ordinary was going on until I took a call regarding a reported break-in."

"Where?"

"Remo Hills area. Big house owned by Charles Gleicher, the news anchorman. He's currently on assignment somewhere in the Middle East."

"And?"

"I notified Johnny and headed to the site. I got there shortly after the security patrol guy did. Johnny hadn't arrived yet. So I started checking it out. The guard and I, we located the point of entry. French doors off the rear patio. I drew my weapon, told the guard to stay put, and went inside."

"And?"

"I heard the sound of a muffled scream. I headed toward it, announcing myself as I did. That's when a man's voice called out he was holding a hostage."

"Who was it?"

"He said something about a young woman."

"And?"

"Johnny arrived and joined me."

"Then what?"

"The guy shot him."

"Excuse me?"

"Caught him in the hip. Twice. Ambulance is on its way. You need to be here, Buddy."

———————————

When I arrived, I spotted the ambulance and a pair of paramedics loading Johnny Kennerly into it.

"What's up?" I inquired.

"Hit twice," the lead paramedic told me. "Right hip and thigh. We sedated him. Alerted the medical staff at Remo General, where we're taking him."

I looked at Johnny, who gazed back at me glassy-eyed.

"Fucking guy shot me. I never even had the chance to engage him. Watch out for this guy, Buddy."

"Thanks, John. I'll get to the hospital as soon as I can."

He nodded.

The ambulance drove off.

"I alerted Al Striar," Dave Balding told me. "He's rounding up whomever he can find at this hour and will be here soon."

"What's with the hostage?"

"I spoke to the perp. Told him everything was all right. Told him to lay down his weapon and release the girl."

"And?"

"He told me to go fuck myself."

"Figures. Where is he?"

Dave led me toward one of the bedrooms. Told me not to show myself. To remain stationed in the archway out of the shooter's direct line of vision.

I called out to him. "Can we talk?"

"Only if you're the boss."

"Go ahead."

"You're in charge?"

"I am."

"I need to get out of here. I need you to arrange it."

"Tell me what you want me to do."

"I want my car."

"Which is where?"

"A block away. Black Accord. Keys inside."

"And once you have it?"

"I want the area cleared so this bitch and I can get out of here."

"What's your name?"

"Why do you want to know?"

"I'm Buddy. I want to know what to call you."

"Jeff. Call me Jeff."

"Jeff what?"

"Just Jeff."

"Okay, Jeff. Let's examine realities for a few moments before we take any action."

"What realities?"

"I'm prepared to make certain you get out of here safely."

"So what's the catch?"

"You exchange the girl for me."

"I'd sooner kill her."

"Listen to me, Jeff. I'm a much better hostage than she is. We'll do a swap. I'll arrange to be handcuffed and leg cuffed and any other cuffed you might want. You let the girl go, and you drive away with me. Simple."

"And if I say yes?"

"You take me to wherever it is you feel safe, dump me, and drive off. Scot-free."

"How do I know I won't be followed?"

"Because then I'd become a dead guy and no one wants that. Think about it, Jeff. The girl for me. I'll be trussed up. No threat to you. We drive away. No one follows. You go to a place of your choosing and release me. Then you escape. End of story."

There was silence for a while.

At last he said, "Okay."

"Okay. I'm going to have the car brought to the driveway in front of the house. My associate will bind me up. At a given signal, you and the girl exit the house and we'll meet at the car."

"With no one else around."

"I'll make certain of it."

"I'll kill you if anyone tries anything cute."

"I'm aware of that."

"Okay."

"I'll holler as soon as I'm in place."

"And all the other vehicles are gone."

"Affirmative."

"All personnel, too."

"Again affirmative."

"Okay."

"Let me speak with the girl."

"Why?"

"To reassure myself of her condition."

"She's heard all this. Consider yourself reassured."

"Are you okay, Miss?"

I heard Jeff murmur, "Say yes."

"Yes," the girl said. "I'm scared."

"Shut up," Jeff said to her.

"Don't be scared. You'll be safe."

No one said anything.

I turned to Dave Balding, and together we exited through the front door, which we left open.

"I don't like this, Buddy."

"It's all right. Go get the Accord."

"You really want me to truss you up?"

"Yes."

"It's too dangerous, Buddy."

"Not really. I've got the element of surprise on my side."

"He shot Johnny. He could just as easily shoot you, too."

"I'm betting he won't."

"I don't know…"

"Help me get ready, Dave. Let me worry about my safety."

Then I gave him my instructions.

Jeff turned out to be a visibly nervous thirty-something who was in over his head. He was standing in the doorway, the girl at his side, holding a polymer-framed Ruger American pistol against her forehead.

"What's *he* doing here?" Jeff said, motioning to Dave Balding. "What's that other car for?"

"The exchange. You hand the girl over to Dave and at that moment, I'll replace her as your hostage. Then Dave and the girl will drive away and you'll be free to load me into your car and escape."

"How do I know you'll do as you say?"

"Because I'm bound and cuffed."

He thought about that for several moments. He appeared fearful of what might go wrong. Then he sighed and after moving the girl in front of him, began to inch toward me.

The girl was crying, which annoyed him. "Quit it," he said and smacked her with his pistol.

Dave nudged me forward. Because my ankles were tethered, I was only able to take the equivalent of baby steps.

Jeff and the girl reached the Accord before Dave and I did. The exchange was to take place at the front passenger door. The girl and I would change places, and then Dave would escort her to his cruiser, place her inside, and drive off.

I surmised Jeff was a loose cannon and from the deer-in-the-headlights look he was displaying, anything was possible. Convincing him that he was in charge was the main challenge.

I tried my best to relax, to appear unruffled, to give him the impression I was compliant and represented no danger to him.

He gave me the once-over, and satisfied I was properly bound and as a result, didn't present a threat, he proceeded with the exchange.

What he hadn't counted on was what Dave Balding and I had in store for him.

As I stepped gingerly in his direction, without warning I suddenly feigned having been tripped by a large stone in the path. I staggered momentarily, lost my footing, and lunged into him, throwing him off balance just long enough for Dave to shoot him in his gun-hand shoulder.

Dave then hustled the girl to his cruiser and summoned the ambulance that was stationed nearby.

Jeff sat where he had fallen, stunned, his shoulder oozing blood. He was in shock. "You lied to me," he wailed.

"Don't you hate when that happens?" I said as the medics hoisted him to his feet and loaded him into their ambulance.

After removing my cuffs and shackles, I stepped over to the girl who was in front of Dave's cruiser. "You okay?"

She nodded, still shaken.

"Who are you?" I asked.

"Jill Nelson," she said. "Charles Gleicher's niece. I'm house-sitting for him."

"Are you okay to stay here?"

"I'm a little shaken. But I'll be okay."

She was an attractive young woman. Late twenties. Early thirties. Wearing a long-sleeved gray T-shirt under dark-blue overalls.

Clearly nervous, she repeatedly ran her fingers through the mane of chocolate-brown hair that surrounded her narrow face.

"I'll make sure there's a squad car with a pair of police officers stationed outside. Twenty-four seven. Give Dave the info, and he'll notify your uncle. We'll make certain you're safe."

"Thanks, but that's not really necessary. He's gone. The threat's over. I'll be okay on my own," she said as a pair of squad cars sped up the driveway.

I nodded.

"You okay?" Dave asked me.

"Relieved it didn't go south," I said. "You did great, Dave."

Dave smiled sheepishly.

"I'm going to see how Johnny's faring. Fill Marsha in on what's gone down. Get Jill settled in the house. Make sure one of the cruisers spends the night here."

He nodded.

I looked around for several moments, then headed for my Wrangler.

NINE

I parked in the visitor's lot of San Remo General Hospital. Built in the late nineteen hundreds, the steel-and-glass edifice bespoke modernity. It glistened warmly in the late morning sun as I hurriedly made my way to the emergency room.

I showed my credentials to the head nurse, who then escorted me to the surgical theatre, where I caught up with Dr. Phil Yalowitz, the noted surgeon and longtime San Remo fixture.

"They're both in surgery," Phil responded to my questions about Johnny Kennerly and the gunman. "Be a while before either of them will be able to converse."

"The prognosis?"

"Good for both. Johnny will have to undergo some serious rehab. He caught one in the hip and one in the thigh. He'll limp around for a spell, but ultimately he'll be fine."

"And Jeff?"

"He's lucky. Suffered only minor damage. He'll be fine. One of the officers has his wallet, by the way. That should ID him."

"I'll assign one of the locals to keep an eye on him. You'll let me know when I can speak with them?"

"I will. How's Burton?"

"Feisty. Angry. Fighting the good fight."

"Someone told me the meds are helping."

"They are."

"But?"

"Let's just say that coming to grips with one's mortality can be disconcerting."

"Tell me about it," Phil said. "I gotta get back to surgery, Buddy. Good to see you."

"Likewise."

On the drive to my father's house, I checked in with Marsha, who told me that Jill Nelson was safely ensconced in the house. "And despite her rather tepid objections, we have a squad car stationed outside. Mostly to ease any anxieties she might suffer."

"Well done," I commended her.

I filled her in on Johnny's condition.

"Sounds like he'll be off the reservation for a while," she said.

"Looks like it."

"It's none of my business, but I'm sensing a big void in the leadership category here in Sheriffsville."

"Bummer."

"I can't imagine who might fill that void."

"Big shoes to fill."

"Hopefully there's someone with feet large enough to step into them."

"You were right, Marsha."

"I was? About what?"

"It's none of your business."

"Oops. I think I hear the other phone ringing."

I knew she was right.

Based upon my father's frame of mind, I was well aware he was in no way up to stepping back into the fray. At least not yet.

I could hear him in my mind's ear referring to me as the *Acting Sheriff*.

And I could further hear him spouting his hooyah about career and the governorship and blah, blah, blah. If I thought I was depressed yesterday, yesterday couldn't hold a candle to today.

I pulled into his driveway, fearfully anticipating what was to come.

He was in the den, surrounded by bookcases filled with leather-bound volumes he had never read. Photos and awards also graced the myriad shelves, along with accumulated gifts and framed, laminated newspaper and magazine articles about him.

His presence in a den primarily devoted to the story of his life completed the portrait of a lion in winter.

"Tell me this hostage-taker you brought down was the thief responsible for all of these home invasions," he said.

"He's not."

"What do you mean he's not?"

"He's not the guy."

"How do you know?"

"Methodology."

"What methodology?"

"This guy, this Jeff, he's a dumb kid who considered himself omnipotent and then stepped in shit. The home invader is a pro."

"You haven't interviewed him yet, have you?"

"Won't matter. He made every mistake in the book. He set off the alarm, and instead of getting out of there, he became entangled with the house sitter. And, to make matters worse, he took her hostage."

"You did good, by the way."

"Thank you. Textbook stuff."

"Why did he shoot Johnny?"

"Fear."

"Without even a word of warning?"

"He saw a black man and acted impulsively."

"Damn."

"Exactly."

He stood and began pacing the room. "What do you think I should do?"

"You're asking me?"

He nodded.

"You know exactly what you're going to do."

"Why would you say that?"

"Don't do this dance with me, Burton. It's unbecoming."

He stopped pacing and stared at me. "Will you do it? It's temporary."

"Not if you announce your intended retirement. Then it becomes political."

"How do you want me to announce it?"

"I don't want you to announce it at all."

"But you'll be the Acting Sheriff."

"I'll be the same deputy I was before. Nothing has changed. I'm back after a short break. In the same job. No announcement necessary."

"Why are you so stubborn?"

"You mean because I won't accept an appointment as Acting Sheriff?"

"Yes."

"Because it won't stop there and instead of just doing the job, I'll be thrust into a spotlight I don't want or deserve."

"And if I disagree?"

"Find another turtledove."

He glared at me.

"Okay. You win."

"It's no victory, Dad. It's what I promised you and what I'll do to help preserve your legacy."

"Without creating one of your own."

"Exactly."

After briefly reviewing with him all I would be doing in the job, I slipped away from the old man's house having donned the mantle of Acting Sheriff. Without the title.

As I headed for the station and the start of a new stage, a wave of sadness swept over me like unexpected nausea.

It would be a couple of months before Johnny came back, and even then he might not be up to taking the reins.

I thought things couldn't get worse.

Once again I was wrong.

TEN

When I wandered in during the noon hour, I found my old school chum Andrew Snyder, the owner of Remo Financial Services, sitting in my office.

Generally neat and well groomed, Snyder was disheveled and distressed, doing his best to suppress his frenetic anxieties.

He looked up when I entered. "Buddy," he exclaimed, "I'm sorry to have barged in like this. You know, unannounced."

His condition alarmed me. Andy and I had attended high school together. Both of us had been influenced and hindered by our fathers. Mine a lawman. His a banker.

"What's up, Drew?"

"I've been robbed."

"Robbed?"

"A cyber theft. Someone or something hacked into my accounts and emptied them."

"Your financial accounts?"

"Investment accounts. Holding accounts. Everything."

"How could they have done that?"

"I don't know, Buddy. But they did. I'm ruined."

"Aren't you insured against cyberattacks?"

"No."

"Why not?"

"I'm a small company. I never imagined I could be vandalized this way."

"How much are we talking about?"

"A couple of million."

"Yikes. What about the FDIC?"

"Washed their hands of it."

"How could they do that? Aren't banks supposedly insured by them?"

"Only in the event of a bank failure. Not a hacked theft."

"Astonishing."

"Indeed. Do you know anything about cybercrimes?"

"No. I'm a Luddite."

"Do you know anyone who does?"

"Why do you want to know?"

"I was told that someone adept at delving…a computer expert…with knowledge of the vast technological underbelly…a person like that could possibly locate the thief."

"If someone like that exists, I assure you I'll find him."

"I'm swamped, so this better be good," Assistant District Attorney Skip Wilder said when, after first refusing my call, he returned it as soon as I mentioned to the person who answered his phone that I knew where he lived and was prepared to go there and beat the crap out of him.

"Cybercrimes."

"Meaning?"

"We've just had one. A doozy."

"You mean there's been a hacking?"

"I do. Involving someone you know, too."

"Who?"

"Andrew Snyder."

"Andy Snyder from high school?"

"One and the same. He's in need of a tech whiz."

"You mean someone adept at computers and electronic devices?"

"Yes. And he needs that person yesterday."

After several moments, he said, "I might know someone. From when I was a liaison to the LAPD. But I hesitate to make a recommendation."

"Because?"

"Like with most millennials, you'd be dealing with a colossal pain in the ass. One who exhibits little or no respect for anything or anyone."

"Who is it?"

"Quinn Anthony. Like the movie star."

"What movie star?"

"Anthony Quinn. Only backwards."

"Wait. Let me get this straight. I'm a little sleep-deprived. His name is Anthony Quinn?"

"Her name is Quinn Anthony."

"Her name?"

Yes."

"You mean he's a she?"

"Yes."

"And her name is Anthony Quinn?"

"Quinn Anthony."

"What kind of name is that?"

"She blames her parents. Claims they thought it would add to her mystique."

"What were they, nuts?"

"I'm not up for this today, Buddy. She has her own company."

"Where?"

"San Remo City."

"Do you have a number for her?"

"Quinn Anthony, Inc."

"You don't have a number?"

"Look it up yourself."

"Why are you being such a jerk about this?"

"You'll find out."

"What's that supposed to mean?"

"Don't say I didn't warn you."

ELEVEN

"Quinn Anthony Inc.," a throaty female voice answered.

"Sheriff Buddy Steel for Quinn Anthony."

"What's it about?"

"Is she there?"

"I'm not prepared to answer that question until I can tell her what it's about."

"I'm a San Remo County Deputy Sheriff."

"So?"

"I'd like to speak to her about a confidential matter."

"Does she know you?"

"No."

"So what's it about?"

"I may have a job for her."

"Doing what?"

"May I please speak with Quinn Anthony."

"You are speaking with her."

I began to get an inkling of what Skip Wilder was talking about. "You're Quinn Anthony?"

"I just said that."

"Is it your nature to be so abstruse?"

When she didn't respond, I added, "Perplexing."

"Is it your nature to be so condescending? I know the definition of abstruse. And yes, it is my nature."

I quickly changed the subject. "I'm told you're tech-savvy."

"Savvy how?"

"Cybercrimes."

"That's not very specific."

"Look, Ms. Anthony. If you're available and seeking employment, perhaps there's a way we can meet and discuss this?"

"Where are you?"

"Freedom."

"I could meet you there."

"In Freedom?"

"For dinner."

"You mean dinner tonight?"

"Yes."

"Where?"

"You know Salty's?"

"Yes."

"Salty's at seven. You buy."

"Okay. I'll meet you there."

"Wait. How will I recognize you? Will you be wearing some kind of ridiculously garish Sheriff's duds?"

"Brown corduroy jacket."

"That's very helpful."

"What will you be wearing?"

"A look of consternation. Make the reservation. Seven o'clock."

She ended the call.

I already knew that Wilder was right.

Located on the Crosstown Highway, Salty's, once a roadhouse haven for truckers and heavy drinkers, has been reimagined into a favored hangout for millennials and Gen Z college students.

Although the place was vibrant and deafening even at seven o'clock, I scored a two-top at the rear, as far away as possible from the commotion.

I spotted her before she noticed me. She was wearing a gray Lululemon sweatshirt over snug-fitting blue tights. A shock of blond curls was tied in a bun and piled atop her head like an outrageous beanie, offering an unimpeded glimpse of her elegant face with its azure-blue eyes and sculpted cheekbones. She wore no makeup. Brown horn-rimmed eyeglasses were her sole concession to nerdiness.

She saw me staring at her and looked quizzically back for a moment. I watched as recognition dawned. She stepped over to the table.

I stood.

"A gentleman," she snorted. "You don't see too many of them these days."

She offered her hand and I took it, surprised by her crusher grip. "That's some handshake."

"You were expecting, what, some kind of wet fish grip?"

She was no sooner seated when a waitress appeared at the table.

"Loquat martini," Quinn said.

"Stella," I said.

"Guac and chips," Quinn ordered.

The waitress nodded and hurried off.

"Loquat?" I queried.

"In season."

"Any good?"

"Only a Gen Xer would ask such a question."

"You mean your choice of drink is generational?"

"Is there any choice that isn't generational?"

"I hadn't really thought of it that way."

"Thereby proving my thesis."

"Talk to me about tech-savvy."

"I presume this means you're changing the subject."

"Probably better than getting stuck in the generational hoo hah."

"I know about you," she said.

"Excuse me?"

"I worked LAPD."

"You were on the nerd squad?"

"I was. Best they had, too."

"So, what happened?"

"You mean why am I no longer LAPD?"

"Yes."

"Rules."

"What rules?"

"Their dumb-ass protocols. Finally it just wasn't worth it. They were burying me in paper. I hated living in LA. My boss was an old-school moron. So one day I quit. I've been on my own ever since."

"Successfully?"

"You're talking to me, aren't you?"

"What is it you know about me?"

"Heartbreaker."

"I beg your pardon?"

"*Bed 'em and dump 'em. No deal Steel.* That's what they called you in LA."

"I never heard that."

"Why would you?"

The waitress arrived brandishing our drinks, a bowlful of guacamole, a side of salsa, and a mountain of chips.

Quinn smiled and raised her glass to me. I touched my bottle of Stella Artois to it. "Is there a chance we could talk a little business?"

"That's why we're here."

I told her about Andrew Snyder's cyber-robbery. "He's likely to go belly-up."

"So what is it you envision for me?"

"How can you help?"

She thought quietly for several moments, then said, "From my experience, the primary method of dealing with cybercriminals is first to identify them. Which, for the average layman, is nigh on impossible."

"And to you?"

"I'm very good at what I do."

"Meaning?"

"What do you know about the dark web?"

"Nothing."

"Would you like a little backstory?"

"About the dark web?"

"Yes."

I nodded.

She downed a guac-loaded chip followed by a large sip of martini. "The dark web is a part of the internet that isn't readily available to normal users and normal search engines. You have to own the anonymizing browser TOR in order to access it.

"Its unsavory business is conducted in secrecy. Identities are unknown. Cryptocurrency is a key element. With it one can acquire any number of illegal items, including credit card numbers and passwords, IDs, drugs, guns, and most significantly, malware that infects computers and paves the way for cyber thefts like the one your friend experienced.

"Anything goes on the dark web, and not everything is as it seems. Scams are prevalent. Purchases are often fraudulent.

Disagreements are legion. Web IDs are suspect. Whistleblower sites abound. It's total chaos. It's amazing anything ever transpires on it."

"Yet it thrives."

"Hooray for capitalism."

"Which means?"

"Widespread corruption."

"So young yet so cynical."

"Come on, Buddy. It was the baby boomers who set the table that the rest of us are now forced to sit at."

"That's your definition of capitalism?"

"You have a better one?"

"You haven't yet said how you could help."

"I can identify the thief."

"The thief who stole Snyder's money?"

"Is there someone else you want me to identify?"

"How?"

"How can I find him?"

"Yes."

"You wouldn't understand. But I can tell you I know my way around the dark web better than anyone. It's why the LAPD hired me. It's why I'm successful."

"Okay. Find him."

"You mean you wish to engage my services?"

"It's amazing how perceptive you millennials are."

"Is that some kind of wisecrack?"

"Take it for what it's worth. And yes, you're hired."

"Terms?"

"Whatever it costs."

"Who will I be working for?"

"San Remo County."

"Not going to happen. I'm not going to work for any county. I will work for you, though. No one else."

"Why?"

"Why you and no one else?"

"Yes."

"Because I like you."

"That's the reason?"

"You have a better one?"

TWELVE

Quinn worked and lived in a small Craftsman-style bungalow in South San Remo County. Her living room was converted into a makeshift office, home not only to herself, but also occupied on a daily basis by a pair of working associates, both of them millennial women.

Computers and TVs and other smaller devices abounded. Quinn and her associates occupied outsized desks, each piled high with un-filed paperwork and overstuffed binders. Although there was an air of chaos to the room, the work appeared to progress with orderliness and efficiency.

We were sitting in the kitchen, amid a forest of yet-to-be-washed coffee cups, glasses, and dinner plates. A pair of obviously well-fed cats awakened, took one look at me, and fled.

A Cuisinart coffee maker was aromatically brewing on the sideboard. An ice maker could be heard disgorging a fresh batch inside the freezer of a double-doored Sub-Zero. A box of vanilla Oreo Thins sat unopened on the table.

"It's not often we have visitors to our little chapel," Quinn Anthony said.

"Thanks for showing me around."

"The customer always gets his way."

"That's your slogan?"

"My lie."

"At least you're honest about it."

She smiled and stood. "I'll be in touch," she said and ushered me out.

———————

On the drive back to Freedom, I checked in with Marsha Russo.

"The dynamic duo called."

"What do they want?"

"A return call, of course."

"Can you plug them in?"

"One moment, please."

She put me on hold and, in short order, came back on the line to announce District Attorney Michael Lytell and Assistant District Attorney Skip Wilder.

"What's going on?" Lytell boomed.

"Regarding what?"

"He's starting," Lytell said to Wilder. "I told you."

"Quinn Anthony," Wilder chimed in.

"She's been hired. Thank you for the recommendation."

"We're in limbo on this cyber thing, Buddy," Lytell said. "There's a whole lot of noise happening. We're under the gun. What does this Anthony Quinn think?"

"Quinn Anthony."

"Yeah, whatever."

"She cited the dark web and claims she can identify the hacker through it."

"The dark web," Lytell interjected. "What a pile of crap."

Wilder overrode him. "Snyder's hunting for an attorney. And whomever he chooses, it's likely to impact us in some way. Probably even involve the FBI. This is a hot potato, Buddy."

"Fingers crossed," I said. "She claims to be expert at cracking algorithms. She exuded confidence. I hope she'll have her result before Snyder engages representation."

"And maybe chickens will fly, too," Lytell interjected.

I heard Wilder cover the phone with his hand and mumble something.

"Yeah, well," Lytell muttered, "I never saw one."

Which was enough to end the call.

THIRTEEN

"Jordyn Yates on line three," Wilma Hansen, the departmental dispatcher, announced over the intercom.

I picked up the call.

"For a guy who's supposed to be off the grid, it's amazing how enmeshed in it you are," she said.

"And good afternoon to you, too."

"How is it trouble always seems to find you?"

"I wish I knew what you were talking about."

"I'm sure you do. But first, what in God's name are you doing back in the Sheriff's office?"

"How do you know I'm back in the office?"

"You answered the call, didn't you?"

"Who told you?"

"It's in the wind, Buddy. What's going on?"

"Home invasions and cybercrimes."

"So trouble does go out of its way to find you."

"Was there something you wanted, Jordy, or did you just call to needle me?"

"Both."

When I didn't say anything, she went on. "My firm was sought out for representation."

"Clients do find their way to you."

"Of course we turned it down."

"Why? You didn't want to go up against the big banks and the FDIC?"

"What are you talking about?"

"Andrew Snyder's cyberattack, of course."

"Who's Andrew Snyder?"

"Quit playing games. He's the victim."

"He's not my victim. I'm talking Jeffrey Brice."

"Who's Jeffrey Brice?"

"Son of Roger Brice. Very wealthy dude. A big deal in retail."

"I'm sorry, Jordy, but I have no idea who you're talking about."

"Guy who got shot. Claims it was racially motivated. Says you lied to him, which opened the way for another cop to shoot him."

"Jeffrey Brice. You mean Jeff?"

"So you do know him."

"This Jeff guy is the jerk who shot Johnny Kennerly. Without warning. In the line of duty. Then he took a young woman hostage at gunpoint."

"Bingo."

"He's suing me?"

"Filed today."

"That's totally nuts. Guy doesn't have a leg to stand on."

"Or a shoulder to pitch with, either."

"What?"

"Incipient baseball player. Some sports physician is certifying that by having been shot in the shoulder, Mr. Brice's career was ruined.

"That's a load of crap. Doc Yalowitz said he'd be fine."

"That may be true, but his big deal father is spending big deal dough for a big deal lawyer to sue you and the county for a big deal settlement."

"You mean you took the case?"

"What are you, nuts? I already have skin in the game."

"What?"

"You, Buddy. I agreed to represent you."

"When did you do that?"

"Just now, of course. And by the way, I'm expecting my client to have dinner with me tonight so as to help prepare his defense."

"Shit."

"Gee, that's a hurtful remark."

"Not you. I can't believe this loser is bringing suit against me."

"Brutal. But at least consider the upside."

"What upside?"

"Following a fabulous dinner during which your incredibly gifted attorney will map out your impeccable legal strategy, there's every chance you'll also get laid."

FOURTEEN

"He's suing me too," Johnny Kennerly told us.

My father and I were sitting in Johnny's room at San Remo General Hospital. He was just starting physical therapy and would remain hospitalized for at least another week.

"Amazing how fast this asshole lawyered up and brought suit," my father said.

"Money talks," Johnny commented.

"And the father has a lot of talking money," I said. "According to Jordyn Yates, the guy buys and sells retail establishments. Big label clothing stores. Regional fast food franchises. Sporting goods outlets. Apparently, he's loaded."

"He thinks he can buy his son's exoneration?" Johnny asked.

"He may think so, but according to Jordyn, the facts won't support it. The kid broke his way in and entered the house with the intention of robbing it. We've got the hostage who will corroborate the whole story."

"Plus he shot me. Twice. Unprovoked."

"He's claiming he did so because you're black. Kid's scream-ing self-defense. Says he was scared you'd kill him."

"I was trying to talk him down."

"Your word versus his."

"So what you're saying is I need to lawyer up."

"You'll certainly require representation," my father said. "I haven't had the chance to speak with the DA about it yet. I'm told he's going to sue the county also."

"What a colossal waste of time," I said.

"Welcome to the new American supermarket," my father said.

"Meaning?"

"Everything's for sale."

"That's a pretty cynical remark."

"You think?"

Dinner turned into a phone conversation. Jordy's sudden change of schedule superseded our proposed dinner, so we made a ten-tative plan to get together on the weekend.

I was at home, having eaten my Lebanese takeout, and was halfway through both an episode of *Blue Bloods* and a bottle of Argentinian Malbec, when Quinn Anthony called.

"I have good news and bad news."

"What's the bad news?"

"My wisdom teeth have to be pulled."

"And the good news?"

"I think I've nailed him."

"The hacker?"

"Yes."

"You only think you've identified him?"

"Okay. Okay. I have him but I haven't yet run all of the algorithms that will confirm it."

"So why are you telling me?"

"Because I already know that the algorithms will bear me out."

"And?"

"Once confirmed, I'll require your consent to take action."

"What kind of action?"

"I knew you'd ask that."

"And?"

"We need to talk about it."

"Okay. When?"

"What are you doing now?"

"You mean this minute?"

"I do."

"It's nearly eleven o'clock. I was contemplating sleep."

"You Gen Xers are so predictable. Early to bed blah blah. So, nighty night. Don't let the bedbugs bite."

"Wait. Wait a minute. You want to talk protocols at this hour?"

"That's why I called. My bad, though. It never occurred to me you'd be nodding out. I suppose you've already had your milk and cookies."

"Has anyone ever commented on what a wiseass you are?"

"Why would anyone say that?"

"Where was it you wanted to meet?"

"Who cares? You're on your way to dreamland."

"What if I'm not?"

"I don't know. I was going to ask you."

"What about the San Remo Biltmore?"

"Oh, great. I should've known that's what you'd come up with."

"What's wrong with it?"

"Clueless."

"Excuse me?"

"You're clueless. Salty's. In half an hour."

When I didn't immediately respond, she went on. "That's where I'll be. I'll wear something sexy so as to keep you awake."

With that, she ended the call.

I sat quietly for a while. Then I got dressed and headed for Salty's.

FIFTEEN

I was lucky to be driving a squad car because parking was impossible. After seizing a spot in a No Parking zone, I inched my way through a crowd of young people in a room blaring with ear-splitting, pulsating music that was antipathetic to any kind of recognizable melody.

Cave-like at this hour, strobe lights illuminated Salty's dance floor that was presided over by an androgynous dude in a tight-fitting red jumpsuit who fielded song requests shouted to him over the din.

I spotted her at the same table we occupied during our first visit. True to her word, she was wearing a flimsy, pearl white Grace dress that revealed a good deal of her amazing body. As before, her sole concession to nerdiness was the tortoise shell eyeglasses she sported mid-nose.

I sat next to her on a built-in leather-bound bench with a leather-bound backboard attached to the wall. Her proximity was disturbing.

She pressed herself against me and whispered, "The better to hear you."

The same waitress from the other day took our respective orders. Hers was a Drambuie Rusty Nail, mine a gin and tonic.

"You have to admit this is a whole lot better than the fucking Biltmore," she said with a smile.

We toasted when our drinks arrived.

"What algorithms?" I asked.

"We could go one of two ways," she said. "Once confirmed, we could blast this guy right out of the sky."

"Meaning?"

"We could compromise his computer and bring it down. Decimate it. Erase everything on it. Render it useless."

"Or?"

"We could do nothing. Monitor him. Leave him alone to carry on his thievery."

"Why would we do that?"

"Lots of reasons, but primarily to possess a window into his operations. If we do nothing, he's unlikely to discover that he himself has been hacked and as a result, won't make any effort to cover his tracks. That way, were he to engage in any shenanigans designed to invade and steal funds or securities, we'd know."

"And what could we do about it?"

"Once I confirm his identity, I can locate him. Tricky but doable. Then we'd have both his ID and his location. You'd be able to track him and ultimately bust him."

"Which do you think is best?"

"You mean what do I advise?"

"Yes."

"My advice is we go back to my place and get naked."

"Regarding the hacker."

"It's up to you, Buddy. Whatever you think is best. I'll have cracked his shell by tomorrow. You can mull on it tonight and decide then."

"And that's it?"

"I didn't say that. The night's young. Me, too. I like you and you like me. Wasn't it you who said you preferred hooking up to settling down?"

"Sounds like something I might say."

"So?"

"Maybe for you the night's young. For me it's already past my bedtime. Plus, I can give you my answer now."

"Go on."

"Don't bring him down. ID him. Locate him. He sounds like the kind of fish I'd like to reel in slowly."

She leaned more firmly into me. "Smart call, Buddy."

"Thank you."

"But the bedtime shit is nonsense. We could be at my place in no time. And I guarantee you'll sleep like a baby."

"Pass. I appreciate the offer, though."

"I wish I didn't like you so much, Buddy."

"Ditto."

SIXTEEN

It was well after three by the time I finally got to sleep, so when the phone rang at just after four, I tried unsuccessfully to ignore it.

"This better be a wrong number," I answered.

"Would that it were," Dave Balding said. "Sorry to wake you, Buddy, but we have another one."

"Another one what?"

"Break-in. Mount Freedom. Neighbor called it in."

"Tell me."

"Says he noticed a suspicious-looking vehicle parked across the street from his house. Unusual because no one ever parks there. When his dog started barking, he got out of bed to see what was going on. No one was in the car. Late-model Infiniti."

"So?"

"So, the guy's awake and he's bothered by the car. Doesn't

want to call it in because legally the driver had every right to park there."

"This is some story, Dave. Is there any chance you could fast-forward through it?"

"Sorry. So later, maybe twenty minutes or so later, guy spots two people making tracks for the Infiniti. One of them is carrying a sack that he tosses into the trunk. Then they drive away. Guy managed to jot down the plate number. He called it in."

"And you took the call."

"Along with a call from a home security outfit."

"Alarm going off?"

"Yes. But here's the rub. It only started going off coincident with the Infiniti's departure."

"Excuse me?"

"The thieves were already in the car when the alarm went off. Meaning it was deactivated during the break-in."

"No one in the house?"

"Correct."

"Sounds like the return of our professionals."

"It does, doesn't it?"

"Is your guy able to identify them?"

"Negative. He's even uncertain as to whether they were men or women. Or both."

"Where are you now?"

"At the house."

"Inside?"

"Yes. With the security guard."

"And?"

"Something strange."

"What?"

"When we were examining the control box, we noticed several drops of moisture. New."

"Did you photograph it?"

"Should I have?"

"Are you at the box now?"

"Yes."

"Is there still moisture?"

"No. It dried."

"What does the guard say?"

"He's baffled."

"Oddly enough, it makes sense."

"How?"

"Wiring can be impeded by temperature."

"You lost me, Buddy."

"A control box function can be negatively impacted by freezing temperatures."

"Meaning?"

"Our professionals may have discovered a way of temporarily disabling an alarm system so that a break-in could take place without triggering it."

"By freezing it."

"It's possible."

"That seems pretty formidable."

"The moisture may be a clue. Make sure the forensics team scrapes up some samples of the dry patch."

"Will do."

"Let me know. And track the plate number, too."

"I did."

"And?"

"Stolen."

"Figures."

"You're amazingly alert for a guy who sounds as if he's asleep."

"You mean I'm awake?"

"Go back to sleep, Buddy." He ended the call.

But I knew that sleep was no longer in the realm of the possible.

At his request, I stopped in to see my father.

I felt somewhat shabby and unkempt, which he noticed immediately. "Burning it at both ends, are we?" the old man commented.

"Don't ask."

"Do you want to fill me in as to what's going on?"

We were on his back porch, both of us sipping coffee, neither of us interested in the finger pastries my stepmother had insisted upon serving.

A brisk wind brought with it an unseasonable chill, and the old man was in his favorite chair, wrapped in a body-blanket.

"We could go inside, you know."

"Let's brave it. I spend too much time inside as it is."

I shrugged. "Never let it be said things in the Sheriff's office are dull. Not only am I dealing with a professionally prepped and meticulously executed series of home invasions, but at the same time I'm being sued by some inane billionaire who's trying to exonerate his idiot son who botched a home invasion attempt of his own."

"This is the guy who shot Johnny?"

"It is."

"They're also suing the department and the county. Why?"

"From what Jordyn Yates tells me, the father's a major litigator. He'll sue anyone or anything at the drop of a hat. It's one of the weapons in his overheated arsenal."

"He thinks he can win?"

"Not a chance he can win. What he can do is get under everyone's skin, stall the proceedings, and make people crazy. My guess is he's hoping that by throwing the kitchen sink at these proceedings he can negotiate his son out of any real penalties."

"How can he do that? His son shot a deputy sheriff. Twice."

"The kid's in trouble. No doubt. But if his legal team can convince a judge that psychiatric treatment could benefit him… He's a first-time offender, and it could have an impact on the judge's ruling. At the end of the day, I'm guessing the old man's going to prevail."

"How?"

"No jail time predicated on a defined period of psychotherapy. Public service requirements. Lengthy probation. Heavy fine."

"So the old proverb holds true."

"You mean: *Money talks?*"

"That's the one."

"We have an even bigger fish in our bowl."

"The cyber thing?"

"It's already a headache. For all the pronouncements made by all of the so-called mavens, cybercrime and its prosecution is still in its infancy. People don't understand it.

"Skip Wilder arranged for me to meet and subsequently engage the services of a former LAPD computer geek who, by means of her nonconventional methods, claims to be able to bring our perpetrator down."

"Is it this Anthony Quinn person I've been hearing so much about?"

"Quinn Anthony."

"Yeah. Him."

"Her."

"What?"

"He's a she."

"No shit. Really? A woman?"

"Your misogyny is showing, Burton."

"How can a computer whiz be a woman?"

"How can a town mayor be a woman?"

"What?"

"You're married to a female mayor. And you, of all people, are questioning the bona fides of a female cybercrime investigator? Shame on you."

"Okay. Okay. So what is this Anthony Quinn actually doing?"

"Quinn Anthony."

"Yeah. Yeah."

"She claims to be on the threshold of identifying the hacker."

"And if she doesn't?"

"This cybercrime thing is a major fur ball. If it escalates, it's going to bite us big-time."

"Sounds like you've got yourself a full plate."

"That's very observant. Do you have any advice?"

He reached over and picked up a pastry.

"Try the prune," he grunted.

SEVENTEEN

And then there was silence.

Like the sky had fallen, halting everything and creating a dead zone in which nothing occurred.

For the first time since I arrived back in town, I slept. Uninterrupted. Untroubled. Unburdened. And I awakened peacefully, not as the result of the insistent ringing of a cranky cell phone.

"What's wrong with this picture?" I queried myself.

I slipped out of bed, hit the loo, and then brewed a pot of Caffè Verona without interference or interruption.

I eased my way through the *New York Times*, then made the bed, straightened things up a bit, and showered.

Still nothing. No frantic updates. No reported crimes. No Quinn Anthony. No nothing. It was like an episode of *The Twilight Zone*.

Finally, I phoned the station.

Wilma Hansen answered.

"Anything for me?" I asked.

"Should there be?"

"I don't know. That's why I'm asking."

"There's nothing I know about."

"No messages?"

"I just said there was nothing."

"You're sure?"

"Is there something the matter with you, Buddy?"

"I guess not."

"So there's no need for me to send someone to check on you?"

"I guess not."

"Should I be forwarding this call to the weirdness department?"

"I guess not. Thanks anyway."

"I'll be saying goodbye now, Buddy. This call has just ended."

Which, in fact, it had.

I sat quietly for several minutes. Then I called Quinn Anthony.

"Quinn Anthony's line."

"Can it. I know it's you."

"Could this be my favorite Gen Xer?"

"Can that, too. What's going on?"

"Regarding?"

"You know what it's regarding."

"I do?"

"Was it your intention to break my chops this morning, Quinn?"

"Once I recognized your voice, it was."

"What's going on?"

"Lunch is going on. Take me to lunch."

I thought about that for a few moments.

"Take me to lunch, Buddy. I'll lift your spirits."

"And you'll tell me what's going on?"

"In minute detail."

"Where?"

"Pick me up at the house in an hour."

———————————

"I don't know why you won't try it?"

We were sitting at an outdoor table at a nearby Carl's Jr., where she was doing her best to convince me to try a Beyond Beef burger, a meatless, plant-based patty, charbroiled and spiced up to look and taste like the real thing.

"Uggh. No."

She wore a V-neck tank top over torn jeans, her mop of streaked blond hair loosely hugging her narrow face.

"You're such a baby," she said. "It's delicious. The least you could do is taste it."

"No."

"Unbelievable."

She laid into her Beyond Beef burger and with the first bite, began emitting animal-like sounds of delight.

I was content with the Santa Fe charbroiled chicken sandwich I happily downed despite her disapproving glare.

We shared orders of fat onion rings and skinny fries. We were both drinking iced coffee—hers vanilla, mine black.

"I've been spending too much time in the dark web," she said between bites. "It's like living in that French movie I saw. *Marseille.* A dangerous underworld of thieves and killers who operate only under the cover of night, in shadows, all brandishing deadly weapons that they use more often than not."

"Sounds like my kind of place."

"It's weird, this dark web. It's all anonymous. Nobody knows who anyone really is. Everyone has a fake handle that is unsupported by reality. Ironically, for such a corrupt and deceitful platform, every transaction relies upon blind faith. It's a universe riddled with shysters and schemers and phishers, all hoping to break codes and expose identities that can then be exploited. Amazing that anything gets done. I've been at it nonstop since our dinner and it makes me feel like I need a bath."

"And what have you learned?"

She finished her burger and, with a look of profound satisfaction, grabbed a couple of onion rings and sat back in her chair. "You have no idea what you're missing."

"Could you please get to the point, Quinn?"

"This hacker person is very good. Not as good as me, but good. I've been tracking the trail of the money. That's the old adage, isn't it? Follow the money? What this hacker has performed is what I refer to as the old *bouncy bally.*"

"The what?"

"The *bouncy bally.* Once he seized the two million, he bounced it all over the world."

"He bounced it?"

"He had painstakingly created a network of hidden IP addresses. Once he set the money in motion, it ricocheted from address to address, all over the globe, quickly becoming untraceable."

"What's an IP?"

"Internet Protocol. A network address for your computer. So the internet knows where to find you."

"I think I understand. Our hacker was bouncing the money from address to address."

"Yes. And at one point during the journey, the lion's share of it exited the ride. Then the balance, a small percentage of the total, continued to bounce. A diversion, really, but at some point, it too, disappeared."

When she spotted my puzzlement, she went on. "Simply put, the money is now sitting somewhere within the system of proxy servers the hacker created. My team is doing all it can to locate it, but for the moment, it's a bear."

"Because…"

"The hacker has gone silent. Zero activity on his account today. Zip. Nada. Nothing."

"Meaning?"

"I'm entering the field of supposition now, Buddy. I'm supposing he's suspending any further activity until two things occur. The first of which is another heist. Similar in execution to the one we're investigating. Followed by a repeat of the *bouncy bally*. Once that's in play, I can locate both the hacker and the moolah."

"How?"

"All I'm going to say is that my team and I have created our own set of malware protocols that are intended to attack and destroy the codes our hacker is employing. I'm confident we'll succeed."

"Is there a timetable?"

"No. As I said, this guy is good. He'll make his move when we least expect it. Which is why we're tuned into him twenty-four seven."

"Yikes."

"Let me ask you a question. It's been on my mind. What do you think the odds are that a millennial and a geezer could make a go of it?"

"Excuse me?"

"You know. A May/September romance. That kind of thing."

"Why would you ask me such a question?"

"Curiosity."

"About a male/female relationship?"

"Only insofar as it might relate to a millennial and a Gen Xer."

"That's some loaded question."

She looked at me for several moments, then picked up the remains of her lunch and dropped it into a nearby trash bin. Taking her lead, I followed suit.

Then we headed for my car.

Once there, I realized she had planted herself directly in front of me. "Would you think about it?"

She was very close, and I was very aware of her.

Then she tenderly caressed my cheek and kissed me. Softly. Her tongue gently moistening my lips.

It was an intense moment that I backed away from. "I might."

"You might what?"

"Think about it. But I'm not promising anything."

"Who asked you to promise anything?"

"Just so we're clear on it."

She stared at me and shook her head. "And here I thought I was the nuttier one."

EIGHTEEN

I was sitting in my office, my back to the door, feet up, staring out the window but seeing nothing.

A soft knock caught my attention and, surrendering my reverie, I found Dave Balding standing in the doorway.

A rugged, wily man with a craggy face, Balding looked older than his years. Following two tours in Afghanistan, he had applied to San Remo in search of a law enforcement position with the county. Having greatly impressed my father, he came aboard the Sheriff's express.

In his early days with the Department, Balding experienced signs of post-traumatic stress disorder. His wife, Laura, recognizing the symptoms, hustled him into psychiatric therapy and made certain he strictly adhered to his twice-weekly sessions.

He suffered a setback last year when, during a large-scale raid on a local drug ring, he was shot in the leg. Fortunately, the wound wasn't severe and he quickly recovered, but the experience served to exacerbate his PTSD. He stepped up his therapy sessions and stoically dealt with his emotional distress.

"Got a minute?"

"What's up?"

He sat across from me. "Forensics."

"What did they find?"

"Traces of liquid nitrogen."

"At the box site?"

"Yes."

"So Lothar was right."

"Excuse me?"

"Lothar Diggins. Cal Poly engineering professor."

"What about him?"

"He confirmed that an electronic device could be impacted by untoward temperatures."

"Such as those offered by liquid nitrogen."

"Yes. But I think we need to do some delving."

"Into?"

"The values of liquid nitrogen, its usages, and its availability."

"And who does that?"

"Nobody better than Marsha Russo."

"Agreed."

"I'll get her started and keep you up to date."

He stood. "Thanks."

As he turned to the door, I stopped him. "How you doing, Dave?"

"You're referring to the shooting."

"I am."

"It was the right thing to do."

"And you did it expertly."

"It was the counting that made it possible. Once you started moving, I started counting. Just like you instructed. When you toppled down on the count of ten, it opened the window to a clean shot."

"I still can't figure it out."

"Why he did it, you mean?"

"Why would a young man like that…rich, privileged… Why would he attempt a home invasion? Makes no sense."

"You interview him yet?"

"It's too top-heavy. Lawyers up the kazoo. Money is involved."

"I heard from Jordyn Yates," Balding said.

"And?"

"She asked a whole bunch of questions. Mostly about my recollection of what went down."

"And you're okay?"

"You know me, Buddy. I don't allow myself to get sucked under by this shit. What went down, went down. The therapy provides a platform for me to deal with it. With my feelings about it."

"And?"

"I'm good."

He reached out and shook my hand. "Thanks, Buddy."

"Unnecessary."

"Not everyone would understand."

"Not everyone would be as courageous as you."

"Not much choice when you consider the alternative."

"No, it's not," I said to Marsha Russo.

We were in my office. She was sitting in one of the visitor's chairs, a yellow pad on her lap.

"You're sure of that?"

"Yes."

"It's not laughing gas?"

"No, it's not laughing gas."

"I could've sworn…"

"Listen to me, Marsha. I know what you're up to."

"Whatever are you talking about?"

"You're not going to get it."

"Get what?"

"My goat. Liquid nitrogen is not laughing gas."

She stared at me dead-eyed. "Whatever you say, Mr. Science Guy."

"Can we please get past this, Marsha?"

"I'm certainly not standing in the way."

"Liquid nitrogen. I want to know everything about it."

"Define *everything*."

"I want to know where and how it's manufactured and distributed. Its form. Its manageability. How does one purchase it? In what quantities? Its high and low temperature range. Its durability. Pretty much everything there is to know about the ways and means of how it's made, marketed, and administered."

"And I'm guessing you want this information yesterday."

"Correct."

"Okay."

"Okay what?"

"I'm on it."

"Good. Thank you. Oh, and there's one more thing."

"No one can know about it?"

"How do you know that?"

"This isn't our first dance, Buddy. I'm very familiar with your protocols. So step out of the way. I'm coming through."

NINETEEN

"The lion roars tonight," Quinn Anthony said when I picked up her call at 2:30 a.m.

"What is it with you and middle of the night phone calls? Have you no consideration for the sleep-deprived?"

"You geezies are always sleep-deprived. Regardless of the time. Wake up, Big Daddy. We've got action."

"What does that mean?"

"Our boy is on the move. And it's not going well for him."

"I wish I understood you."

"You do understand me. You just don't want to admit it."

"Please, Quinn. I was asleep here."

"Our hacker launched an attack on the Harbor Credit Union. Seeking to swipe their assets. Mostly pension funds they manage for a handful of labor unions."

"And?"

"Boink."

"Excuse me?"

"Firewall. He slammed into it."

"So the raid was unsuccessful."

"Insofar as stealing Harbor's assets, it was."

"There's more?"

"Our hacker got royally pissed off."

"How do you know that?"

"Because he immediately attacked the personal accounts of Harbor's principal executives and investors."

"And?"

"More boinks."

"So, what is it I'm missing?"

"Our guy's weakness has been exposed. Now's the time to take him down."

"What does that mean?"

"Harbor Union wasn't just a shot in the dark, Buddy. If it was, he wouldn't have known who the execs were or how to gain access to them."

"Go on."

"We think he was emboldened by his success in hacking Andrew Snyder's accounts. It raised the stakes for him. So much so that he dug deeper into the dark web and likely made a significant purchase.

"The dark side traffics in the theft and subsequent sale of all kinds of private information. Mostly personal stuff such as email addresses, credit card numbers, savings and security assets…you get the drift. This stuff isn't cheap but, depending on a phisher's needs, it's often worth the price."

"So you think our hacker bought stolen names and addresses?"

"I do. Remember that movie studio incident? Couple of years back. Sony, I think it was. Not only did hackers decimate their systems, they also compromised thousands of personal accounts. Same is true of other cyber break-ins."

"And the information contained in those accounts was then put up for sale?"

"Exactly."

"So what is he so pissed off about?"

"We believe the information he bought was polluted."

"Meaning?"

"It was old and compromised by antiviral security measures that had been specifically developed to defy it."

"So what he bought was worthless."

"And costly. Plus his investment is irretrievable."

"How much are we talking about?"

"Well, if recent marketplace quotes are still holding, I'm guessing in the neighborhood of a hundred and fifty bitcoins."

"In dollars?"

"In today's dollars, approximately eight hundred thousand."

"Eight hundred thousand dollars?"

"Yes."

"Why would he spend so much?"

"He believed he was hitting pay dirt. Because of the Andy

Snyder loot, dollar signs were rolling around in his head. But he made a fatal mistake. He trusted without verifying. So instead of buying gold, he bought dross."

"And?"

"He's scrambling. He knows he fucked up."

"And you want to do what now?"

"Bury him."

"What does that mean?"

"Take him down. Now that he's revealed his network, I say we wipe him out. Raid it, take whatever we can, and then blow it up."

"Which will be to our benefit because?"

"I smoke him out and snatch his spoils. You grab him."

"How soon?"

"As soon as you give me the word."

"Consider it given."

"You know, Buddy, you might want to consider coming over here."

"Now? At 2:30 in the morning? Are you nuts?"

"Yes, now. But the jury's still out on the nuts part. Inasmuch as the cyber-shit is about to hit the cyber-fan, you might want to see how this stuff plays out in real time. Once our pal realizes he's a victim, he's bound to make a whole bunch of mistakes. One of which will be his undoing. Considering your newfound involvement in my universe, I thought watching it unfold might heighten your understanding."

"Now?"

"Now's when the game is about to shift into high gear. Plus, and I hate to say this, I think I know you well enough to predict that you'll never get back to sleep. So, instead of just lying there fretting, come be with me. You may learn something. And even better, you'll be with me."

"You're very enticing, Quinn."

"And that's just for openers."

TWENTY

She let me in and gave me the once-over. "You look tired."

"I can't imagine why."

She grinned. She was barefoot, in a lightweight cotton kimono worn over a pair of men's pajama bottoms.

She led me to the living room/office, where two Apple iMacs, both displaying rapidly changing data, were ablaze on her desk.

"Coffee?" she inquired.

"Black."

She filled a cup from a stainless steel carafe and motioned for me to sit beside her.

"What's going on?" I asked.

"We're watching the playback of a recording my team discovered on the hacker's dark site. He made it in real time when he found he'd been robbed.

"On one screen, he's voicing his complaint to the seller, who's not responding. On the other, he's retracing the money trail."

"What money trail?"

"The money he glommed. Andrew Snyder's money."

"How does he do that?"

"This is where it gets good. For the moment, he's on the dark web. Examining the theft step-by-step. Watch the numbers. See how they're changing?"

"Yes."

"Those numbers are the equivalent of a series of snapshots. A photographic road map of the manner in which the money moved from its original location to its entry into the algorithm that will eventually move it to its current location."

"So are you saying the money is about to move from one cyber-protocol to another?"

"Yes. Very good."

"How does it do that?"

"Maybe this will clarify it for you. Pretend the money is a metaphorical rubber ball that rolls through a hollow tube until it encounters a blockade that stops it.

"In this particular case, based on the algorithm our hacker either wrote or more likely purchased, the so-called blockade senses the arrival of the ball, then instructs itself to lower the blockage. Which allows the ball to transition into another tube, this one with a different trajectory."

"I think I get it. The so-called blockade is the transition point where the money switches from the dark web to the internet."

"Bingo."

"So, what is it we're watching now?"

"A replay of the original theft. The hacker recorded it. My team found it and copied it."

"And in the replay the money hasn't changed locations yet, right?"

"Right. But it's about to. Live and in person. And when it happens, we'll have our answers regarding the hacker."

"How so?"

"We're about to see how so. The metaphorical ball has arrived at the metaphorical blockade."

"And?"

"Did you see it?"

"Did I see what?"

"The dark web algorithm just transferred the money from the dark web to the internet."

"You mean the legitimate internet?"

"Yes."

"I didn't see it."

"Not to worry. But as of this moment, in our hacker's protocols, the money is wending its way through a predetermined series of stops and changes that will eventually deliver it to where it will come to rest."

"The *bouncy bally?*"

"Exactly."

"And we're watching the journey?"

"We are, but it's no longer necessary."

"Because?"

"When the transfer occurred, the sender's IP address was momentarily revealed."

"Why momentarily?"

"Because the moment it hit the sender's address, it immediately leapt into the morass of other addresses that transported it. There was literally a split second between receipt and transfer. Enough time for us to photograph and identify the hacker's address. That information is now being analyzed and will shortly provide the hacker's name and location."

"How can you do that?"

"Protocols and algorithms we designed specifically for that purpose."

Quinn's iMac suddenly went dark. A flashing circle lit up the center of the screen. Then it burst into light and a notice appeared.

She studied it carefully. Then a quizzical look appeared on her face.

"What?" I asked.

"Holy shit," she muttered.

"Holy shit what?"

"I should have known."

"Known what?"

"It's not America-based. The point of internet origination is El Salvador."

"So?"

"It's cartel-connected." She shook her head. "It's a game changer."

I looked at her quizzically.

"There's one other thing," she said.

"Which is?"

"Our *he* is a *she*."

"Excuse me?"

"The hacker's female."

TWENTY-ONE

For the first time since I'd met her, Quinn appeared disheartened. She became withdrawn and contemplative. It was as if I wasn't there. She started moping around the house, pacing from room to room. I followed her.

"What?" I asked.

She stopped pacing and looked at me. "She could be anywhere. And even if I were to locate her exact whereabouts, the playing field has become uneven."

"Is speaking in metaphor generic to your generation?"

"Don't start, Buddy."

"Don't start? This may be the first time a Gen Xer ever had the upper hand with you."

"Don't count your chickens too fast, big guy," she sneered.

"What's changed?"

"You know damn well what's changed. We're now playing a lethal game."

"Because?"

"The cartel is involved."

"So?"

She glared at me but said nothing.

"Listen, Quinn. Prior to this revelation, the game we've been playing has always been a big question mark. What you've just discovered is what's been lurking beneath the surface. The hacker may be cartel-supported, but she's still a hacker. Regardless of her associates.

"The stakes may be higher than you thought, but they're now defined. Categorized. And they're even more up your alley because we still require the information you profess to provide—that is, unless you're too scared to continue."

"Fuck you, Buddy."

"How lyrical."

"I mean it," she said, working up a head of steam. "I don't need your sarcasm to egg me on."

"What's the problem then?"

"There is no problem."

"So, level or not, you're still on the playing field."

She stepped over to me. "You know what I like most about you, Buddy?"

"Uh oh. I like you, too, Quinn."

"You have a girlfriend, don't you?"

"Why would you say that?"

"You do. I know you do."

"She's not really a girlfriend. I mean she's a friend with whom I was once involved. We hadn't seen each other in ages. Then we started working together. And we stepped over the line. And although nothing's defined, we're friends again. Close friends."

"With no commitments?"

"You know me and commitments."

"Will you make love with me?"

"That's a perplexing question."

"Only because you're making it so. I'm not asking for any commitments. No promises. No tomorrows. I'm in no position to see past the now."

She sighed. "You're such a jerk. Let me put it this way. I want to go to bed with you. Is that so wrong?"

"I don't trust it, Quinn. I don't trust myself. Looking at you is like looking into an emotional mirror."

"Albeit a cracked one."

"Exactly."

"I'm not going anywhere, Buddy."

"Neither am I."

"So?"

"I need some sleep."

"You can sleep here."

"Not with you in such close proximity."

"I promise to leave you alone."

"I don't trust that either."

"Is there anything you do trust?"

"Coffee."

She sighed. "You want some coffee for the road?"

"I thought you'd never ask."

TWENTY-TWO

I couldn't rid my mind of the idea that the cyber theft had been perpetrated by a cartel-related operative. Hopefully, it was a onetime occurrence. But were it to become endemic, San Remo County could be in for some rough sledding.

Quinn could go just so far. She'd learn the identity the hacker intended for her to learn. No lone wolf. Who the thief really is and with whom she's associated is now more troublesome. Which is less Quinn's problem and more mine.

I needed to upgrade my knowledge of current Southern California gang activity as it relates to cybercrimes. So I phoned Special Agent Paul DeSavino, the FBI's liaison with the LAPD, a pal from my days in LA.

"My luck," DeSavino bleated when he picked up my call. "A blast from the past. I was wondering when you'd get around to ringing my chimes."

"What does that mean?"

"It's been whispered you hinterland bozos have been rudely awakened to the exigencies of cyberspace."

"Whispered?"

"Actually sung from the rooftops. Quinn Anthony's antics don't go unnoticed for long."

"How so?"

"You know what, Buddy? I think this conversation is bigger than a phone call. Let's just say we're aware of the Snyder dustup and are as curious as you with regards to its origins and intentions. Let's break some bread and discuss it face-to-face."

"You mean I have to watch you eat?"

"Is this a great country or what?"

————————————————

We met for dinner at a favorite of Paulie's, Gravina Malibu, a family-owned coastal *ristorante.*

They knew him there and once we were seated, the owner presented us with an excellent bottle of Chianti. Paulie ordered the homemade pappardelle with wild boar ragù, I the chicken parmigiana.

He produced an oversized black bib which he affixed to his neck with a flourish. "I'm done ruining my shirts," he said with a laugh.

He was a large man with a large personality. Nearing sixty, he had remained in good shape, a gym rat who worked out every day. His fashion was Hollywood casual, a navy cashmere V-neck worn over pressed blue jeans. His narrow face with its aquiline nose and piercing green eyes was invariably brightened by his wide-mouthed, toothy grin.

"You caught yourself a handful," he chided.

"You're talking about Quinn, no doubt."

"No doubt. She was the scourge of the LAPD when she was here. Gifted. Talented. Smart as a whip. Crazy as a bedbug."

"So you knew her."

"She sort of ran the show here for a while. Her technological expertise was and still is a wonder. She had no equal. She was legend down here. You heard the story about her and the Police Academy?"

"What story?"

"You're going to love this. Given the rise of cyber-technology as a weapon in the gang-world arsenal, the LAPD created a special unit to investigate and prosecute cybercrimes.

"Candidates with extraordinary technological skills were recruited nationwide and a number of the most talented enlisted. Among them, Quinn Anthony.

"Although slender and disarmingly slight, she took her assignment seriously and worked diligently, not only to heighten her technological prowess, but to strengthen herself and elevate her corporal skills as well.

"The Police Academy's physical training program was run by Lieutenant Mike Marcus. Big Mike. An oversized bear of a man who had held the job for decades. An avowed misogynist, he believed a woman's place was in the kitchen and not on active duty with the LAPD.

"As a result, the process was pure hell on the handful of women who underwent it. Big Mike claimed that a more forceful and intensive training regimen was necessary to create tougher and more adept female officers. Women who could stand up to whatever challenges the street presented.

"But any number of candidates fled the program due to the terror wrought by his ceaseless bullying. Our dear Quinn experienced his torturous techniques firsthand and was disquieted by them.

"He had singled her out for his so-called *treatment*. She became his go-to scapegoat and he belittled and humiliated her at every turn. But he seriously misestimated her.

"As opposed to being intimidated by him, she diligently studied his methods and techniques in search of vulnerabilities. She found one in the hand-to-hand combat training. The exercise included a staged confrontation between a female cadet and Big Mike himself, one in which he played the role of an assailant.

"It was the cadet's task to overcome Big Mike by employing the judo-like techniques he championed…balance, agility, speed, and inexorable force.

"When Quinn volunteered to oppose him, Big Mike giddily set out to demolish her. But he was unprepared for her swiftness and devastating countermeasures.

"When he leapt at her from his attack crouch, she sidestepped him and as he blew past her, she dived onto his ankle and wrenched it in such a way as to rupture his Achilles tendon.

"Screaming in pain and unable to stand, Big Mike was seriously disabled.

"Although she made any number of apologies, a self-satisfied smirk appeared on her face when the paramedics loaded him onto a gurney and sped him off to a nearby urgent care facility.

"He never returned to the physical training unit. The tendon grew back but would never again support his weight in the manner it once had.

"Quinn attended his retirement celebration, saluted him smartly, and left before the tributes began.

"Following Big Mike's departure, the program underwent serious change. It now shows great respect for women cadets and goes out of its way to help them develop their combat skills.

"Having opened the door to a fair deal for women, our pal Quinn is still revered and respected in the corridors of the LAPD."

"That's some story."

"I told you." Paulie smirked as he dove into his wild boar ragù.

"Tell me about what's going on in gangland," I said. "Who's perpetrating cybercrimes? Who might be operating in my neck of the woods?"

"We're still dogged by MS-13," he said between bites. "They pretty much own SoCal. They have a few rivals and on occasion the roof still gets raised. You know, dead bodies in dumpsters. Drive-by shootings. Beheadings. Classy shit like that.

"But the cyber operatives are mostly nerdy types whose expertise is valued by the cartel bosses. Most of whom are technologically clueless."

"So who's dominant?"

"The most prominent of the lot is Los Perros. The Dogs. They operate under the umbrella of the Salvadorians, whose primary enterprises are extortion, human trafficking, drugs, and weapons. An El Chapo–type kingpin called Chuy Sanchez calls the shots."

"Choy Sanchez?"

"C.H.U.Y. Pronounced *Chewy*."

"He's the boss?"

"Yes."

"You're omitting something, aren't you?"

"Rumor and innuendo."

"Come on, Paulie. Let me in on it."

"I'm not vouching for this, but it's in the wind that Chuy Sanchez's kid is the brains behind the burgeoning cyber-theft enterprise. Everyone envisions a big cyber future, and the chieftains are reliant on tech nerds to escort them into that future. Chuy's kid is one of them. Very talented. Allegedly the apple of his eye."

"So?"

"The kid's team refers to themselves as Los Perritos, the Puppies, and their stomping ground now appears to be your territory."

"How do you know?"

"We've got a few agents on the ground. Implants. Not directly associated with the Puppies, but connected with the Dogs."

We finished our dinners, and Paulie signaled for the dessert menu. "You still got that amazing tiramisu?"

"Tiramisu. Zabaglione. Zuppe inglese. How about I fix you a sampling of them all?" the owner offered.

"Kudos," Paulie said. "Make sure to bring something chocolate. And two spoons."

"Don't be expecting me to share this sugar transfusion with you."

"Suit yourself. But you have no idea what you'll be missing."

"You know, Quinn said that same thing."

"What was it you were denying yourself?"

"A fake meat burger."

"You mean a Beyond Beef burger?"

"Yeah."

"You're a gastronomical cretin. You do know that, don't you?"

"It's been rumored."

"Do you still smear mustard on salmon?"

"Maybe."

"I rest my case."

I smiled.

"Be wary, Buddy. Knowing you, I'm guessing you're intent upon attacking this cyber business. And I promise to help in any way I can. But the rub here is that Chuy Sanchez is totally devoted to his kid. And God help whoever challenges her. Catalina Sanchez. A feral cat amid a litter of docile puppies."

TWENTY-THREE

I was once again jarred awake by the ringing of my cell phone. I mumbled some kind of greeting.

"Did I wake you?" Marsha Russo asked, the hint of a snicker in her voice.

"Not at all. I was reading."

"Liar."

"Why is it you phoned, Marsha?"

"Which do you want first?"

"The good news."

"There is no good news. There's been another home invasion. Dave asked me to call you."

"Because?"

"He was too afraid he might wake you up."

"Where?"

"Freedom Hills. Doc Wynan's house. He's lecturing in Arizona."

"Same M.O.?"

"So says Dave."

"What else?"

"Liquid nitrogen."

"Go on."

"First of all, Dave's going to have forensics run another test. But assuming it is liquid nitrogen, I can answer a few of your questions."

"Okay."

"It's for sale in bulk for commercial usages, and over the counter for personal ones."

"So I could buy it, say, at Walmart?"

"I haven't checked that particular outlet, but you can buy it on Amazon. For any number of usages. Most frequently wart removal."

"Amazon?"

"Yes."

"So it's not traceable."

"Doesn't look like it."

"What's its freezing point?"

"Minus three hundred and sixteen degrees. Fahrenheit."

"Yikes."

"Freezes them warts right off of you. You have warts, Buddy? If so, we could remove them and at the same time solve the home invasion crimes."

"Marsha…"

"You ever see a frozen wart? I know I haven't."

"Marsha…"

"Must be a snarky looking little sucker…"

"Marsha…please."

"What should I tell Dave?"

"Run all the drills. He knows what to do."

"How do we find this guy, Buddy?"

"It just became harder."

"Like one of them frozen warts."

"What do you advise?" I asked my father.

"There's no such thing as a perfect crime."

"I didn't ask your opinion, I asked your advice."

We were porch lounging on a sun-drenched afternoon. Lemonade was chilling in an ice-filled pitcher. The Sheriff was in jeans and a short-sleeved shirt.

"You know, Buddy, you catch more flies with honey than with vinegar."

"Will you be publishing these homilies?"

"First tell me your plan."

"Ratcheting up the search for the stolen property."

"Because?"

"Our home invader is several steps ahead of us. And he doesn't seem to be making any mistakes."

"So?"

"I want to raise our side of the game," I told him. "I need Marsha to study the inventories of the stolen property and identify the items of singularity and value. I can already pinpoint several of them. Like the ones that belonged to that basketball player.

"We've got six break-ins, including yours, with more surely to follow. We need to ally ourselves with insurers and attorneys who are knowledgeable about fencing operations and property retrieval. We have to take sufficient enough action to alert our perpetrator that we're coming after him."

"My opinion?"

"Go on."

"That's the right call," the old man said. "You have anyone in mind?"

"You mean someone who might help us find the stolen property and identify those who've been peddling it?"

"Yes."

"I'm thinking a national law firm. And a prominent insurer. Those who might have prosecuted fences in the past. Aware of the nature of the game and how to play it."

"Such as?"

"Jordyn Yates, for openers," I replied. "Merriweather & Harris. Branches in Los Angeles and other key cities that count."

"M & H is a big-ticket item. Who pays?"

"The department. With City Council approval."

"Risky."

"Necessary."

"How do you go about getting this approval?"

"I don't. You do."

"Me?" my father exclaimed.

"Of course you. Who else?"

"What if I said no?"

"Come off it, Burton. The chances of you saying no are somewhere between zero and zilch. Go get 'em. We need Jordyn on the case ASAP."

"I haven't said yes and already I'm under pressure."

"Let me know when it's done."

TWENTY-FOUR

"Here's one you haven't heard before," Dave Balding said when I answered his call.

"That sounds ominous."

"Listen to this, Buddy. I just received a call from Charles Gleicher."

"The owner of the hostage-taking house?"

"One and the same."

"And?"

"He just got home."

"So?"

"He called to report a break-in. And a rather large theft."

"At his house?"

"Yes."

"Didn't his niece tell him about it?"

"You ready for this?"

"What?"

"He has no niece."

"Excuse me?"

"No niece. No house sitter."

"So who was the girl?"

"Good question."

"Is there a good answer?"

"There's no answer."

"That's my bad. I should have dug deeper."

"It was what it was, Buddy. She was very credible. In any event, she's vanished."

"Vanished?"

"As in disappeared. *Adios*. Kaput."

"How do you know?"

"Jeff Brice."

"You mean the guy who took her hostage?"

"Him."

"You spoke to him?"

"I called him. Obviously, I surprised him."

"Why would he know about the girl? She was allegedly Gleicher's house sitter."

"Are you ready for this, Buddy?"

"Go on. Surprise me."

"She's his girlfriend. Or at least she *was* his girlfriend."

"How in the fuck could that be?"

"Another good question."

"And the answer?"

"He clammed up."

"What?"

"He realized he'd made a mistake by telling me anything, so he told me to talk to his lawyer and hung up."

"And?"

"I called you instead."

"What's all this about?" Jordyn Yates asked when she picked up my call.

"You heard?"

"Just."

"And?"

"I may be able to help."

"I hoped you might."

"It seems odd."

"It's got me floundering."

"That's an attractive image."

"Do you think he'll talk to you?"

"I'm pretty sure it can be arranged."

"And the girl?"

"What girl?"

"Jill. Jill Nelson."

"What are you talking about?"

"Jeffrey Brice."

"Jeffrey Brice? You mean the hostage-taker?"

"Of course I mean the hostage-taker."

"What does he have to do with our trying to connect you with a stolen property trafficker?"

"What?"

"A fence. Isn't that why your father contacted our firm? Something about a backdoor approach to locating stolen loot and a home invasion suspect."

"I'm talking about Jeffrey Brice telling Dave Balding that Jill Nelson was his girlfriend."

"His girlfriend?"

"That's right."

"How could that be? She was the one he held hostage."

"Exactly."

TWENTY-FIVE

As per my instruction, Sheriff's Deputies Al Striar and P. J. Lincoln detained Jeffrey Brice at his father's cottage in the San Remo hills.

As Striar explained to him, Brice wasn't actually being arrested. He was being brought in for questioning. As such, he was denied a phone call and was delivered to a police precinct in South Freedom, where he was detained in one of its basement cells.

I arrived at the station and went directly to a small conference room, where I checked the video-recording device that Striar had set up on this side of the room's one-way glass window.

Acknowledging that everything was in order, I signaled for Jeffrey Brice to be brought in.

He was plenty unhappy. He glared at me. "I want a lawyer."

"I'm sure you do. And you'll get one. Just not yet."

"You have no right to hold me like this."

"Listen to me, Jeff. I've detained you for questioning. Which can go easy or hard. You do well and you go home. All I want is some information."

"What kind of information?"

"The Jill Nelson kind."

"I don't know anything about her."

I stood, moved my chair back, and headed for the door.

"Wait. You're not going to just leave me here."

I stopped and looked at him. "Jill Nelson."

He thought about it for several moments. "Okay. What do you want to know?"

"Who is she?"

"I love her."

"Tell me about it."

"I met her in Santa Barbara. At a party. In some coastal mansion. She was popping down shrimps two at a time like she hadn't eaten in a while. I watched her. She was pretty great-looking. When she noticed me watching, she gave me the finger.

"When I didn't walk away, she speed-ate four more shrimp and headed outside toward the pool deck. I followed.

"Finally, she asked what I wanted, and we talked. She was obsessed about the house we were in. She said it had so many valuable things in it. Looking me right in the eye, she said she'd love to rob it."

"And you took her seriously?"

"I didn't know how to take her. But I sure wanted to take her to bed."

"Did you?"

"Not that night. But we arranged to see each other again. I told her about my father's house in San Remo, and she said she wanted to visit it. That was when we started."

"Started how?"

"Dad was in LA. We were alone in the house. She was intrigued by it. Now that I think of it, more by it than by me. She told me she wanted to fuck me in every room. Over the course of the next few days, she did. Nothing like that ever happened to me before."

"And you didn't think it strange?"

"Strange? It was unbelievable."

He sat quietly for a while. As if experiencing some kind of reverie. Then he looked at me. "Things weren't always good between me and my father after my mother died. I could never live up to his expectations. He kept me on a short lead. I was a pain in the ass and he wanted me in check. He had no truck with my interest in a baseball career. He wanted me to learn his business. Entry level. No Fancy Dan stuff. So I drove his old Lexus. I was the assistant manager of one of his chain boutiques. Learning the ropes, as he liked to say."

"Go on."

"She suggested we rob one of the nearby houses. She had looked around and noticed that a number of them were empty. Second homes. She told me she knew how to disable alarm systems, which would clear the path for us to get inside and clean up.

"She said she could gain access to the floor plans and layouts of any number of the houses by simply visiting various city and/ or county realty offices and, under the guise of being a broker, ask to examine the files of the various homes she claimed were being listed for sale or lease."

"And you went along with it."

"I did. But reluctantly."

"And?"

"We succeeded a few times. It was my idea to do only the houses we knew for sure were empty. Celebrity homes. Ones where the occupants were away. Information readily available online."

"Charles Gleicher, for instance."

"Exactly."

"So what went wrong?"

"It was my bad. I bought the wrong coolant. We had been in the house for about three minutes when the alarm went off. We couldn't get out in time. We got caught. And then I shot that guy. I'm really sorry about that. I panicked. He scared the shit out of me."

"Who thought of the hostage thing?"

"Jill did. On the spot. She was so pissed off at me. She had masterminded the whole thing, and then I fucked it up. She didn't believe we would be caught. Or that I would get shot."

"So, where is she?"

"Gone. She had been living with me. In the cottage. But by the time I got back there, she had stolen everything of value and split. No forwarding address. Cell phone no longer in service."

"Any ideas as to where she might have gone?"

"None."

"Do you know where she's from?"

"No."

"Do you know anything about her?"

"I know Nelson isn't her real name."

"What is?"

"I haven't the slightest idea."

TWENTY-SIX

I arranged for Jeffrey Brice to be moved to another police station in what Johnny Kennerly referred to as "Buddy's Jailhouse Shuffle."

I wanted to keep Brice under wraps until I completed my investigation. I knew that with his father's legal team swarming, I'd never get another chance.

I phoned Judge Ezekiel Azenberg and asked if he might expedite a search warrant for the Brice cottage. I instructed Marsha Russo to round up a forensics team and dispatch them to that location. I found Dave Balding and arranged for him to meet me at the cottage. We were all there in less than an hour.

We gained access through a poolside door, and when the security provider responded to the sounding of the alarm, we presented our warrant.

The purpose of all this was to provide the forensics team an opportunity to dig up traces of Jill Nelson's DNA. They were to scour the bedrooms and the bathrooms first, then follow suit in other rooms.

There was no assurance we'd hit pay dirt, but if we could grab any of her DNA, it would be our best chance of identifying her.

After a brief walkabout at the cottage, I left Balding in charge and departed.

The irony of both suspects in two separate criminal investigations being millennial women wasn't lost on me. Neither was the fact that women were also key players in the investigation of these crimes.

Times change, I reminded myself.

When I entered the station I was greeted by Wilma Hansen brandishing a fistful of phone messages.

"You only need to read the top one," she exclaimed.

"Why?"

"Because they're all from the same two bozos."

"Let me guess."

"You win."

"But I haven't guessed yet."

"Shall I ring them for you?"

"I suppose there's no avoiding it."

"Like death and taxes," she said.

Once in my office, I spotted the red phone light blinking and I picked up the call.

"We know what you're up to," ADA Skip Wilder pronounced.

"And it has to stop," DA Michael Lytell added.

"Good afternoon, gentlemen," I said.

"Listen to him," Lytell said to Wilder. "He's sliming us."

"Sliming you?"

"You know what I'm talking about, Buddy," Lytell said. "Where is he?"

"I have no idea what you're talking about."

"I'm already worn out by him," Lytell said to Wilder. "Aren't you worn out by him?"

"Cut the crap, Buddy," Wilder said. "You're dancing the jailhouse shuffle and we know it. Release him immediately."

"He confessed."

"Confessed to what?"

"Aiding and abetting in the commission of several home invasions and thefts."

"That's why you arrested him?"

"I didn't arrest him. I brought him in for questioning."

"But you're hiding him?"

"I'm not finished questioning."

"Listen to me, Buddy," Lytell bellowed. "The wrath of the California justice system is about to come crashing down on us. Let him go."

"I'll take it under advisement."

"Are you listening to this numbskull?" Lytell said to Wilder. "He's taking it under advisement."

"You have to release him," Wilder said.

"Okay."

"You have to do as Skip says," Lytell said and then stopped himself. "Wait. What did you just say?"

"I said okay. I'll release him."

"Now," Wilder said.

"Okay."

"Where is he?"

"Where do you want him delivered?"

"To his house. That's where we want him delivered. To his father's cottage."

"That's not possible just now."

"Why not?" Lytell said.

"I've got a forensics team there."

"What for?"

"DNA samples of the principal suspect in the home invasion crisis."

"Why there?"

"Because Jill Nelson was living there. With him. I learned that earlier today. So before the entire world shows up and pollutes the place, I need the chance to gather some DNA evidence."

"And you have a proper warrant?"

"I do."

"Then deliver him here. To this office."

"Might take a while."

"Six o'clock."

"I'll try."

"No 'I'll try.' Six o'clock. End of story."

TWENTY-SEVEN

The bedside clock told me it was just after 3:00 a.m. and the phone was ringing.

"Damn," I said by way of a greeting.

"It hit the fan," Quinn Anthony proclaimed.

"What?"

"Three significant thefts in less than an hour. We're lit up like a Christmas tree here."

I made a half-hearted attempt to sit up. "Tell me."

"The San Remo Savings and Trust. Wally Gordon's Mercedes dealerships. All three of them. And my favorite, the Genuine Foods holding account."

"Why is it your favorite?"

"Because their so-called fresh groceries are frequently on display beyond their sell-by dates. I can't tell you how many times I got stiffed."

"So, what do you propose we do?"

"We have options. I think you should hightail it over here so we can figure them out and decide."

"You look like hell," she said as she welcomed me.

She was barefoot and had on a pair of shorty pajamas that immediately caught my attention.

"Coffee?" I asked.

"I just poured it."

"What do I have to do to get it?"

"Follow me."

She led me into the kitchen, where a steaming cup awaited me on the table.

I sat. She sat.

I sipped.

She spoke. "Apart from the bank, I know how she was able to swipe the other two accounts. Neither of them bore any kind of serious security. She cherry-picked the account numbers and passwords and cleaned them out in no time."

"And the bank?"

"A bunch of stupids. Accessing their security protocols was like taking candy from a baby. The thing about cybercrime is no one really understands it. I mean some people do, of course. But many of the geezer-run companies are nonbelievers. Their attitude is 'It won't happen here.'"

"How much?"

"Collectively, over a million. The bank was the hardest hit."

"Did you trace it?"

"Off the grid."

"Meaning?"

"It played bouncy bally until it vanished."

"Retrievable?"

"Only by apprehending the hacker."

"Catalina Sanchez."

"I'm unable to locate her."

"Why?"

"There's a wall around her. Every attempt I make to gain entry is met with a *boink*."

"Even though you know her identity?"

"I may know her identity but not her coordinates."

"And how do you find them?"

"That's where our options come in."

I followed her into the living/work room. None of her associates were present. She motioned me to a chair next to her in front of the two iMacs.

"So, what's the best option?"

"We head directly for the bedroom and I jump on your bones."

"And the second best?"

"If it were up to me, I'd infect her bouncy bally network. And to that end, me and my team have developed a malware algorithm that will slash through her network like a hot knife through buttah."

"My team and I."

"Excuse me?"

"You said *'Me and my team.'* It's *'My team and I.'*"

"Thank you for the grammar lesson, Professor Geezer."

"To what end?"

"I presume you're talking about the malware attack."

"To what end?"

"Well, for one thing, we eliminate her network and in the doing, hide the money."

"Hide it how?"

"Once the original network is erased, so to speak, the only way the money can be accessed is through the new protocols we'll insert. Which have their own entry requirements. They'll provide the only access to the cyber parking lot where the money has been stashed."

"Didn't Catalina prepare for such an invasion?"

"Once the money exited the dark web and entered the net, the security measures she had in place changed. The new security protocols were easily hackable by me and my team. My team and I. I and my team. Regardless of how inviolate they may have appeared to her."

"Because?"

"We were well-prepared for this inevitability."

"And the money?"

"We have two choices."

"Go on."

"One, we return it from whence it came. We're hailed as

cyber heroes and me and my team are deluged with more business than we can handle. My team and I, that is."

"Choice two?"

"We dangle it in front of Catalina and offer her a way to
retrieve it."

"Ransom?"

"You could call it that."

"And if she bites?"

"Game over."

"Meaning?"

"Once we find her, you bust her."

"And?"

"My team and I are hailed as cyber heroes and are deluged
with more business than we can handle."

I mulled that over for a bit. Then I said, "While I would like
nothing more than to see you and your team become the stuff of
legend, there's still a problem."

"Which is?"

"Catalina is cartel-protected. Her old man is some kind of
kingpin."

"So?"

"There's a risk factor here."

"Meaning?"

"We could be facing dismemberment and death."

TWENTY-EIGHT

"You might want to think twice about it," Paul DeSavino commented.

I was in my office. He was in his.

"Meaning?"

"You're likely to meet opposition from Chuy Sanchez. Especially if bringing her down means any kind of criminal charges and/or incarceration."

"Which it well might."

"You're stepping out of your safety zone with this, Buddy. Although you're experiencing her malfeasance in a small-town environment, you won't be on the receiving end of small-town retribution. This guy won't fuck around. He'll send his goons out to annihilate you."

"So you're suggesting I should simply throw in the towel?"

"Hand it off."

"To whom?"

"To us. You did your job. Now turn it over to the Feebs."

"How likely are you to get involved?"

"You could ask your old man to talk to Ross Patton about it."

"The FBI regional director?"

"Yeah. Him."

"And you think he'd step into the middle of this?"

"Uncertain."

"Isn't he beset with bigger fish to fry?"

"You'd think."

"So what good would it do to talk to him?"

"It couldn't hurt."

"To what end?"

"To the not-getting-yourself-killed end."

"There's a risk factor. You could get yourself killed," my father bellowed.

It was an unseasonably chilly day, and we were in his den with a fire roaring.

"What are the odds of that really happening?"

"We're talking Los Perros here. And the Salvadorian cartel. You think they'd hesitate to erase you? You and your Anthony Quinn friend."

"Quinn Anthony."

"Yeah, whatever. Listen to me, Buddy. I'm going to turn this over to Ross Patton."

"And if he's lukewarm about it?"

"It's still his headache."

"And you think San Remo County will continue to develop and prosper in the face of unchecked cybercrimes?"

"We don't know that to be a fact."

"Then go talk to Ross Patton. But don't be surprised if he tosses it onto the back burner. Particularly with more significant crimes happening in more important places."

"Let's hear what he has to say before we go off half-cocked, shall we?"

"You're the Sheriff."

"Thrice elected, too."

———————

"All right, I spoke to him," my father said when I picked up his call. "You were half right."

"Meaning?"

"He says he'll look into it."

"And?"

"It's complicated."

"Come on, Dad. What did he say?"

"He wants us to sit on it for a while."

"What's a while?"

"He didn't say. Told me there's been a rash of cyber thefts in both LA and San Diego. Seems like the gangs have embraced this new phenomenon and are climbing all over themselves in their efforts to steal as much as they can as fast as they can."

"So?"

"The numbers are bigger than the ones we're dealing with."

"How much bigger?"

"Millions bigger."

"So?"

"The FBI is heavy into recruitment, but it's not so simple. There aren't that many qualified techies out there."

"Lucky us, then."

"What lucky us?"

"We have Quinn Anthony. She's already cracked the existing codes and is standing ready to bring the hacker down. If she can do that, in light of the San Remo cyberattacks, it will be a boon for our county."

"Not at the expense of her life."

"We'll certainly put safety measures into effect."

"At what cost?"

"At whatever the cost. You know what I don't like about this?"

"What?"

"The idea that a Sheriff's department can be scared off because of an alleged threat by gangs. It's chicken shit."

"It won't be chicken shit when some *pistolero* is holding you at gunpoint."

"Bring it on."

"Are you losing your marbles?"

"I'm beginning to think that maybe I am."

TWENTY-NINE

Once again I found myself wishing I was anyplace else but here.

It seemed like it was only days ago that I was on my own, with no responsibilities other than to prowl the beaches and mountains and come to grips with where my life is headed.

And here I am now, occupying a position I thought I had successfully abandoned, dealing with issues I believed I had ditched. I guess I fooled myself.

The cybercrimes fiasco was beginning to look more and more like an orphan. The recipient of insincere levels of concern with no concrete support.

Unlike the bigger counties where there is a genuine interest in thwarting these kinds of crimes, out here in the so-called sticks, people don't fully understand what's happening and are clueless as to how to combat it. Just as Quinn said.

Then there's this home invasion scourge. Further complicated by the oddball connection between the scion of a family of significant wealth and an inveterate home-invader who's vanished.

These issues, germane to the well-being of San Remo County and its inhabitants, are weird enough to have engendered an uncharacteristic level of uncertainty on the part of those in charge.

My father is growing more distant and less interested.

The District Attorney's office doesn't grasp the nature of cyber offenses and how to deal with the perpetrators.

The Feds, overwhelmed by the glut of cyber thievery, are hesitant to add more to their already overloaded plate. So, with regards to their rural jurisdiction, i.e., San Remo County, which they consider to be small potatoes, they've adopted a wait-and-see approach, rationalizing fear as the main reason for their inertia.

Be afraid of the gangs. Don't move too fast. Death and destruction are lurking.

In the face of those fears, the only person who appears to support taking action is me.

And I've got only a single ally, a headstrong millennial who understands the predicament and wants to tackle it head-on.

Despite being a woman, she reminds me in so many ways of the younger me. Footloose. On the make. Sexually hungry in a startlingly compelling manner.

I was sitting in my living room, illuminated by the random shards of moonglow peeking through the blinds, a half-empty bottle of Beefeater's on the table beside me.

"How in the hell did I get into this mess?" I asked myself. "And how in the hell do I get out of it?"

The phone jolted me from my reverie.

"She struck again," Quinn Anthony announced when I picked up the call.

"Where?"

"Freedom Township. She emptied the coffers."

"What?"

"She invaded the town bank accounts and snatched it all."

"This isn't going to sit too well around here."

"You know what I truly love about you, Buddy?"

"What?"

"You're the master of understatement."

I brushed past her remark. "Can it be recovered?"

"It depends."

"On what?"

"Whether or not you're willing to unleash me."

"Meaning?"

"You know what it means. It means retaliation. Risk and reward. Let me do what I need to do, Buddy."

"It worries me."

"What does?"

"Your well-being. What happens if you succeed and it unleashes the demons?"

"You mean the cartel demons?"

"Yes."

"I guess we'll just have to find that out."

THIRTY

"DNA," Marsha Russo uttered as she dropped into the visitor's chair across from me.

A woman of a certain age, Marsha was particularly energized this morning. A longtime veteran of the Sheriff's Department, she's a great favorite of my father, who affectionately refers to her as his "shtarker."

"What about it?"

"They found a match."

"Go on."

"Prints were identical to those of a young woman already in the system."

"Who is she?"

"Prints match with a Jill McDonough. Last known address in Santa Barbara, CA."

"Is the address still active?"

"Good question."

"Is it?"

"I think so."

"What, I think so?"

"My SB police pal says real estate records indicate it's a one-family home owned by an R. J. McDonough."

"Did he check it out?"

"She."

"Did she check it out?"

"I didn't ask her to."

"Because?"

"I didn't think you'd want to sound an alarm. This Jill person has already fled once. Be a shame to lose her again—if she's there, that is."

"Want to take a ride?"

"With you?"

"To Santa Barbara."

"What are we waiting for?"

————————————

It took almost half an hour to make the drive to number 40 Colony Drive East, the alleged home of Jill Nelson. *Née* McDonough.

It was a white and black Minimal-Tudor cottage, representative of mid-century American home design, located in a residential neighborhood amid a number of similar residences.

We parked down the street and made our way on foot.

Marsha slipped around back to ensure that if Jill were there, she couldn't flee. I climbed two steps to the front door and rang the bell.

After several moments, it opened and standing there before me was Jill Nelson.

"Shit," she said and tried to slam the door in my face. My foot prevented it.

"So nice to see you again," I said.

"Yeah, well, fuck you, too."

Her cheeks a bright red, she glared at me defiantly. She wore an oversized gray sweatshirt over torn blue jeans. She was barefoot.

"You might want to put on some shoes," I said.

She gave me the finger.

"I'd hate to haul you off to the hoosegow without shoes. Be pretty uncomfortable for you."

Again she tried to slam the door, but I grabbed her arm and pushed her back into the house.

"Back door," I said.

"What about it?"

"Take me to it."

"Fuck you. No."

"You know, this would be whole lot easier if you were at least somewhat cooperative."

I squeezed her arm harder and escorted her to the rear of the house. Once in the kitchen, I opened the door for Marsha.

"A real pain in the ass," I told her, pointing to Jill.

"Allow me," she said.

She slammed a pair of handcuffs on the girl. "Come with me, honey. We need you to pack a few things and get some shoes on those feet."

Without waiting for a response, Marsha hustled her out of the kitchen and disappeared upstairs.

I made tracks for the cruiser and moved it onto the driveway of the McDonough house.

Marsha led Jill to the car and the two of them climbed into the back seat.

A pair of dog-walkers were staring at us.

I waved to them, backed out of the driveway, and headed for San Remo.

THIRTY-ONE

She was none too happy when Marsha deposited her in one of our holding cells.

"Let's keep her on ice for a while," I said. "I need to question her before the hordes descend, and I don't want anyone getting to her before I do."

"You think hordes will descend?"

"Once they learn she's here."

"What hordes?"

"The hordes of legal demons who will be engaged to secure her freedom."

"How long will we be keeping her?"

"For as long as it's necessary."

Marsha sneered and left to tend to Jill.

I punched the number for Chanho Pineda into my cell phone.

"You free?" I asked him.

"You mean now?"

"Yes."

"Aw hell, Buddy. What is it this time?"

"Chuy Sanchez."

"You're kidding."

"Do I sound like I'm kidding?"

"You ever hear the old adage, 'When you play with fire you burn to death'?"

"No. Where are you?"

"I'll meet you in Sutter's Park."

"Half an hour."

"I'm going to regret this, aren't I?"

"Just like always," I said and ended the call.

I had known Chanho Pineda since high school. Although we hadn't attended the same one, we were both gym rats, devoted basketball players, who ardently made the rounds of the local courts.

Frequently, we were on the same team in our various pickup games. Three on three. Our third was generally Johnny Kennerly.

Brought up on the so-called wrong side of town, Chanho was subjected to recruitment attempts made by local gangs. But as a star athlete, the gangs respected his neutrality and he walked among them with impunity.

After graduating from Cal State, which he attended on an athletic scholarship, he embraced the life of a community relations operative.

He counseled young Latinos and helped many of them find their footing. He met with gang leaders in an ongoing effort to establish a lasting peace among them. He was a role model as to how a first-generation immigrant might integrate into the society for which he or she had left their native country.

Or as Johnny Kennerly termed him, "He's one of the good guys."

He was now on the Governor's Community Relations Advisory Council and a force in the statewide effort to promote immigration and integration.

He was seated on a bench in front of Sutter's Park Lake, his face turned to the sun. I sat next to him.

Without even opening his eyes, he said, "That was a short-lived sabbatical."

"Don't remind me."

"And here I thought I was rid of you for a while."

"Life's a bitch, isn't it?"

"I'm afraid to ask why I'm here, Buddy."

A rangy player in his youth, Chanho had been a big man with a wide wingspan and a broad beam. He'd beefed up in his later years and was now fighting a losing battle with the scale.

"I want to meet Chuy Sanchez."

"Great idea. Good luck with it."

"No. I mean it. I need you to arrange it."

"What makes you think I could ever do such a thing?"

"Don't play dumb, Chanho. Just make it happen."

"If I could, which by the way I can't, under what auspices would I arrange such a meeting?"

"Under the safety of his daughter auspices."

"Meaning?"

"She's generated a major brouhaha in San Remo County."

"How?"

"She's a cybercriminal. Committing mayhem and thievery under the alleged protection of her father. Some serious charges can be pinned on her. Charges that will surely earn her a lengthy imprisonment."

"So?"

"It worries me that such a sentence might further inflame the tensions between Los Perros and the San Remo Sheriff's Department. Before it comes to that, I'd like to see if I can negotiate some kind of truce."

"How?"

"I don't know. Maybe a little tête-à-tête somewhere. Just the two of us. Chuy and me. I have a proposal I'd like to make before things go bonkers."

"Tell me."

"No."

"You won't tell me your proposal?"

"Correct."

"Why the fuck not?"

"Listen, Chanho. The less you know, the better. What I need is for you to inform Chuy Sanchez of the gist of this conversation and ask him to meet with me sometime within the next twenty-four hours."

"Never gonna happen."

"Make it happen, Chanho. Then later we can get loaded and celebrate how you and I managed to avert what might easily have become a big fat motherfucker of a bloody-assed mess. Okay?"

He stared at me. "I'll look into it."

THIRTY-TWO

"She's looking everywhere for you. She's out of her mind," Marsha Russo said when I answered her call.

"And you're referring to?"

"Your stepmother, the mayor. She's totally nuts."

"Tell me something I don't know."

"I'm going to get off the phone now, Buddy. But before I do, allow me to recommend that you call her."

I called her.

"Do you know about this, Buddy?" she erupted.

"The cyber theft?"

"Yes, the cyber theft. They took everything."

"I heard."

"What in the hell do we do about it?"

"Where are you?"

"At home."

"I'm on my way."

She had the door open even before I got out of my cruiser.

She was dressed as if for a high-style event—black Gucci suit, immaculate coiffure, expertly applied makeup, fully prepared for her close-up in the off chance she might stumble upon a media conclave.

"Everyone's clamoring for an interview," she said as she ushered me inside. "I have no idea what to tell them."

We made our way to the kitchen, where my father was sitting. He, too, was dressed for business. He glared at me. "How could this have happened?"

"I hate to say I warned you about it."

"He warned you?" Her Honor exclaimed, glancing at my father.

"This cybercriminal is using San Remo to help make her bones," I said.

"Fuck her bones," my father bellowed.

"Please, Burton," Regina chided. "Let me handle this. What does it mean, Buddy?"

"The county is experiencing an increasing number of cyber thefts. In answer to which our department has engaged the services of a highly qualified technical expert whose job it is to track down and identify the perpetrators."

"With no obvious results," the Sheriff said.

"Not true. We're close to taking action."

"What good does this do me?" Regina asked. "And how do I explain it to the press?"

"You handle it in your normally masterful way."

"Shit," my father said.

"Burton, please," Regina said.

"We've identified the hacker and believe we can achieve the return of the stolen funds. I'm guessing we'll settle it one way or the other within the next twenty-four hours."

"Is that what I tell the press?"

"I think you need to be noncommittal with the press. If it becomes necessary, tell them it's under investigation and clam up about everything else."

"Clam up?"

"In your normally masterful way."

My father snorted.

Regina appeared deflated. "I wish I understood all this cyber nonsense."

"Now you know how I feel," the Sheriff said.

"I'm on this, Regina," I said. "I'm not promising anything, but off the record, we're close to resolving it. You need to keep it under wraps until then."

"So what do I tell the press?"

"You tell them nothing."

"That's easy for you to say. They'll crucify me."

Again my father snorted.

"Then for at least the time being, avoid them."

"And how do you propose I do that?"

"You might try laying low for a while."

"How would I do that?"

"I'm sure you'll find a way."

THIRTY-THREE

"Are you done with the cooling-her-heels protocol?" Marsha Russo asked.

We were in my office, and the late afternoon sky was darkening. "Has anyone come looking for Jill?"

"Not that I know of."

"I have doubts anyone will."

"Why?"

"She's a wild child. Keeps her own counsel. She may be living in her parents' house, but I'll bet they have no idea as to her comings and goings."

"So what do you want to do?"

"Find out what's happening with her."

"When?"

"Now's as good a time as any."

"Are you going to keep her here?"

"If she's the architect of the home invasions…as well as a perpetrator…she'll have earned herself a ride on the District Attorney Trolley."

"How likely is it?"

"That she's the perp?"

"Yes."

"Beats me."

We adjourned to the conference room where, escorted by Deputy Al Striar, Jill Nelson McDonough joined us.

Sullen and wan-looking, she sat across from us, glaring. "He wants to kill me."

"I assume you're talking about Jeffrey Brice."

"Of course I'm talking about Jeffrey Brice. I'm certain that when he couldn't find me himself, you became his primary option."

"You're suggesting he wanted me to locate you so he could kill you?"

"He set you up."

"What is it I'm not understanding here, Jill?"

"I don't know what he told you, but whatever it was, it was lies."

"He told us you were his girlfriend."

"Of course he told you that. I bet he also told you the whole thing was my idea."

"He did."

"And you believed him?"

"We had no reason not to."

"Fucking police. What a sorry joke you guys are."

"How about you tell us your side of the story?"

She sighed deeply and slumped down in her chair. "I was in Santa Barbara. Staying with my father. Down on my luck, as it were. I'd been working for a start-up chemical manufacturing outfit in LA. Secretarial stuff. Getting by. Then it went belly-up. They owed me a few weeks' pay. Good luck trying to collect it.

"So I moved back home to regroup. I'd been there for maybe two, three weeks when my old man got invited to this party in the hills. He couldn't go that night so I snatched the invite and I went. That's where I met Jeff.

"I was mostly minding my own business. Chowing down on the buffet. I noticed him staring at me. Finally, he made me uncomfortable so I went outside to get away from him. He followed.

"When I asked what he wanted, he got all mushy and fed me some line as to how attractive I was. He told me he was living at his father's San Remo estate, bored silly. Then he lowered his voice and told me he was a thrill seeker mulling a way to commit the perfect crime.

"He tried to get me to go home with him, but I refused. He asked for my number and—stupidly—I gave it to him. He called twice that night and again the next day. Said he wanted to show me his father's estate.

"I'd been having issues with my father, and I guess I wasn't in my right mind. So I went with him and as promised, the place was amazing. He said he was living there alone and invited me to join him. By then I had convinced myself he was kinda cute, so I accepted his invitation."

"And?"

"He showed me around. Led me to one of the guest rooms and told me it was mine. Took me out to dinner. All very up-and-up. But once we got back to the house, all he wanted to do was fuck.

"I resisted at first but I knew ultimately I'd let him, so I let him. And it was okay. I mean he wanted to do it all the time and sometimes I had to fend him off. But we were alone in this great place. We watched movies. We swam. We cooked. You know, we lived the high life. We fooled around. And then he told me his plan."

"Which was?"

"He said he wanted to rob a house. Break in and steal stuff."

"If he was so well-off, why would he want to do that?"

"For the thrill of it."

"He wasn't worried about getting caught?"

"He said if that ever happened, his father would come to his rescue. He was dead serious about it. He had selected a few houses in Santa Barbara. He had gotten information from some real estate agency about the layouts. Said he knew where the valuables were kept.

"When I asked him about alarm systems and security mea-sures, he said he had this idea about how to disable them.

Something to do with slicing wires. That's when I made my big mistake."

"Which was?"

"I told him about liquid nitrogen."

"The freezing compound."

"Yeah. How at the right temperature it could freeze wires."

"Security alarm wires?"

"Any wires."

"And he liked it."

"Liked it? He went ape shit. He made me tell him how he could get his hands on some. When I told him he could pretty much buy it in any hardware store, he damn near had a heart attack."

"So?"

"He bought some almost immediately and experimented on the alarm system at his house. When it worked, he could hardly contain himself."

"So what happened?"

"He wanted to make a few dry runs. On houses in Santa Barbara. Said they would be practice for when we made really big scores in the greener pastures of San Remo."

"So what happened?"

"We did a few. In and out fast. We got away with it. But then he got scared. Said Santa Barbara was too far from home. He was afraid the cops would get on our trail."

"Hence San Remo."

"He wanted to start big there. The Sheriff's house in Freedom.

Said he'd read somewhere the Sheriff and his wife would be in Palm Springs for a week."

"The Sheriff's my father."

"It was your father's house?"

I nodded.

"Holy crap."

"What happened next?"

"We did it. And we got away clean."

"So then what?"

"We pulled off a few more and then it turned south."

"At the Gleicher house?"

"Yeah."

"Why?"

"Turns out the dope hadn't put enough liquid nitrogen on the wires and the alarm went off. We had bagged a shitload of stuff and he wanted to take it with us. I said for him to just leave it and let's get out of there. He said no. We argued.

"Then this black guy turns up. One of you. So the dickhead fires at the guy. Hits him twice. Then we hear sirens and he comes up with this bright idea to pretend he's holding me hostage. The rest you know."

"And now you think he wants to kill you?"

"I know he does."

"Why?"

"Fear."

"Of?"

"Of me contradicting his story. The news coverage was pretty comprehensive. You know, 'Rich Kid Robs Other Rich Kids.' Shit like that.

"Then I find out he's pleading not guilty. Claims it was all my idea. My plan. His lawyers make him out to be my victim. So, it dawns on me that if I weren't around to deny it, he could contend I was the ringleader.

"It was no surprise his old man bailed him out. So now he's free. Guilty as shit. But free. And he knows I can nail his ass.

"So he figures out a way to get you cops involved in trying to find me. And now that you have, he'll come up with a way for me to die. Some way that won't look like murder."

She withdrew into herself for several moments, deep in thought. Then she looked up and said, "It's his only move. With me alive to provide the truth, he knows he'll go back to jail.

"But if the defense was to paint a portrait of him as the victim of a conniving, thieving woman who isn't around to defend herself, seduced by her into shooting a police officer, for which he's crestfallen and remorseful, by the way, the chances are good he'll get either a reduced sentence or probation or no sentence at all. Getting me out of the way is his ticket to freedom."

"So it was all lies."

"About how he said it went down?"

"Yes."

"You're damn right it was all lies. And now I'm totally fucked."

"Because?"

"One way or the other, he wins, I lose."

THIRTY-FOUR

"So what did you make of that?" Marsha asked when we were back in my office.

"The question is which of them is lying?"

"Which do you think?"

"I think it's likely they both are."

"You think they're both lying?"

"I do."

"So what happens next?"

"We shuffle her. She's definitely a flight risk."

"For how long?"

"Until I can bring Jordyn Yates up to speed. Then she and the DA can make the call."

"Is there someplace where you want to shuffle her?"

"How about Pyongyang? What if we shuffled her there? Let Little Rocket Man look after her."

"I wish you were as funny as you think you are. Where?"

"You decide. Then use your magical powers of coercion to convince her we're protecting her from Jeffrey."

"And you think she'll buy that?"

"She will if you're good enough to sell it."

The intercom buzzed. "Chanho Pineda on line two," Wilma Hansen announced.

"Wonders never cease," Chanho said when I picked up the call. "He'll see you."

"When and where?"

"That was what he asked."

"How about tonight? Nine. Ten. Whatever works best for him."

"Where?"

"Tricky. What do you think?"

"He doesn't like to be seen in public. But I have a nutty idea. What about the San Remo City Hall parking lot? By evening it's deserted. We set up a table and chairs. In the open. No recording devices. No filming. Just two guys sitting outside shooting the shit on an early summer evening. With guards posted to protect them."

"Not bad. You want to sound him out about it?"

"Sure."

"Thanks, Chanho."

"Wait until it's over before you thank me. Then I can remind you how you owe me big-time."

"Tell me again," I said to Quinn Anthony.

I was in my office. She was in hers.

"The algorithm we developed can locate the whereabouts of the money. It can't actually liberate it. That's something law enforcement would have to do."

"Is the money now housed in some kind of banking or financial institution?"

"In an unmarked account."

"Where?"

"In the Cayman Islands."

"Can it be moved?"

"Only by the hacker. Cat something."

"Catalina Sanchez."

"Her. If that's her real name."

"Can you tell when the money is moving?"

"Yes."

"Is it?"

"Not yet. Would you care to fill me in on what's happening, Buddy?"

"I will. Tonight. One way or the other."

"Meaning?"

"Just leave it at that."

"What do you mean *leave it at that*? I'm hanging by a thread here."

"I'll be more definitive following a meeting I'm about to attend."

"That's great. I'll just sit here, twiddling my thumbs."

When I said nothing, she implored, "Give me a hint."

"No."

"Give me a hint or I'll never talk to you again."

I thought about that for a few moments. "It's likely we'll be exercising the blooey option."

"You mean you'll want me to take her down?"

"If things go as I think they will."

"And you want me to keep tabs on the dough?"

"Yes."

"And I'll hear from you tonight?"

"Likely."

"When tonight?"

"Assuming I'm still alive, sometime around midnight."

THIRTY-FIVE

As in a duel, the seconds arrived first. The parking lot had emptied, allowing for the placement of a table and two chairs in the center of the area.

It was close to 7:30, and the evening was cool but not cold. The sky was darkening, but the stars and the occasional chopper were visible.

The agreed-upon protocols called for two reps from each side to position themselves at a preordained perimeter within eyesight of the principals but outside of hearing range.

Each rep was armed and stood shoulder to shoulder with an opposite-side rep…one pair in sight of the chair that would house me, the other in sight of the Chuy Sanchez chair.

Satisfied all was in order, the signal went out for the principals.

Chuy arrived in a black Mercedes SUV. The driver got out and studied the area. Then he opened a back door and Sanchez stepped out. He, too, perused the surroundings and then stood behind the chair that was marked for him.

I entered on foot and walked quickly to the table and stood behind the chair that was mine.

We stared at each other.

He was a squat fireplug of a man, standing at what I assumed to be about five and a half feet tall. He wore a black suit but was tie-less, revealing a glimpse of his neck and the colorful tattoos emblazoned on it. He glared at me out of guarded, serpentine eyes that reflected both cunning and hostility.

I reached out to shake his hand, and after a moment of uncertainty, he took it.

"With respect," I said.

He nodded.

We sat.

"I'm here because Chanho asked me to see you," he opened. "Why?"

"I thought perhaps together we might be able to ward off what promises to be a goodly amount of grief."

"Meaning?"

"Your daughter."

He said nothing.

"She's gotten herself into trouble with the law."

"How so?"

"I hope it's not your intention to play dumb here, Señor Sanchez."

Again he said nothing.

"I want to propose a deal. One that would serve your interests as well as those of San Remo County."

"I'm listening."

"She cleans up her mess and leaves town."

"In exchange for?"

"Her freedom."

"Define mess."

"She targeted the county and stole a significant amount of money from a handful of citizens and institutions. She riled everyone. The Sheriff's Department. The LAPD. Even the FBI. She stirred up quite a hornet's nest. They're all planning to come after her, and when they catch her, as they surely will, they'll crucify her. I'm offering her a way out. She returns the money she stole. And her operations in the county cease."

Following an uneasy silence, he said, "She's a very headstrong young woman."

"I don't really care."

"What if I'm unable to convince her?"

"You're kidding, right?"

His lips curled into a sardonic snarl.

I remained silent.

He remained silent.

"Do we have a deal?" I finally asked.

He didn't respond.

I stood.

"Don't let it be said I didn't warn you."

He stood.

"You're misguided, Mr. Steel, if you think there's a win in this for you."

"Then we're both misguided for the same reason."

I turned to leave.

"I have a proposal for *you*," he said.

I turned back at him.

"Stay out of this. You're playing a losing hand. It's not us who should be packing up and leaving town."

"Is that some kind of threat?"

"It is what it is."

I flashed him my own dead-eyed stare.

"Arrogance is no excuse for stupidity, Mr. Steel."

"Stupidity is no justification for pigheadedness, Mr. Sanchez."

"You'll regret this," he said and signaled for his car.

THIRTY-SIX

My first call was to Quinn Anthony. "Go for it," I said to her.

"The whole enchilada?"

"Yes."

"Now?"

"Yes."

"Excellent call, Buddy."

"There'll be repercussions."

"There always are."

Then I phoned FBI Special Agent Paul DeSavino. "Are you ready?"

"I assume you're referring to the series of events we discussed earlier."

"I am."

"Okay. When?"

"As soon as possible."

"I'm guessing that in Buddy-speak, it means immediately."

"It does."

"You know it could backfire."

"I do."

"And you're aware of what might happen if it does."

"I am."

"You're vulnerable Buddy. Hell, we both are."

"It's the chance we agreed to take. Besides, it has everything going for it. Not even Big Chuy could predict we'd hit him thrice."

"I'm assuming you've taken measures to protect yourself? And Quinn?"

"I've got a plan, if that's what you mean."

"Good. Try not to fuck it up."

"I appreciate your vote of confidence."

By the time I arrived at Quinn's house, she and her team had already achieved their goal.

"We obliterated her site. It no longer exists. We grabbed all of the data, copied it, then blew it up along with everything else."

"The money?"

"Stashed in an account at Rothberg & Sons Financial Services, Inc., on Grand Cayman island."

"And you're certain we can access it?"

"Only coincident with when she accesses it."

"Has she reacted?"

"Not that we can detect."

My cell phone rang. It was Marsha Russo. "How'd it go?"

"As expected."

"And my marching orders?"

"Also as expected. Unleash the security force. I'll need Judge Azenberg to sign the warrants and the extradition papers. I'd say wheels-up by not later than midnight."

"Done."

I ended the call and turned back to Quinn. "Are you ready?"

"Never readier."

"And the drill?"

"The computers have been removed. Paperwork, too. My team is minutes away from leaving. The local cops are on their way to begin the stakeout. Say the word, and we're out of here."

I excused myself and called Paul De Savino. "Mission accomplished," I said.

"Armageddon?"

"Total."

"The dough?"

"As we discussed. And you?"

"Both locations are operational."

"Troops in place?"

"At each location."

"When?"

"As soon as the joints are jumping."

"Meaning?"

"We want to take down as many johns as we can. In addition

to the girls and the staffs. I'm thinking we'll strike in about an hour, hour and a half."

"And the port?"

"At dawn. They're loading the trucks now. We'll hit them as soon as they attempt to leave the dock. Boom. Boom. Sanchez won't know which way to look first."

"You still think he'll show?"

"At the dock?"

"Yes."

"Very good chance. He likes to keep an eye on things. Especially when there's a big payday involved."

"Like tonight."

"Exactly."

"And he won't be distracted by the busts?"

"He'll be annoyed but he won't lose focus. Them opioids are worth a fortune."

"I'll call you," I said.

"I'll be waiting."

THIRTY-SEVEN

It was time to clue my father in on the events of the day. Packed and ready to leave, Quinn and I stopped in to see him.

It was late and he was in his pajamas and bathrobe, brandishing a large glass of Jim Beam. The three of us sat at the kitchen table.

"What's up?" he asked, keeping a wary eye on Quinn.

"We've unleashed a joint action…us, the FBI, the LAPD, and the San Diego PD."

"Relating to the cybercrimes?"

"Yes."

"Go on."

"Quinn and her team have already destroyed the hacker's website. She's tracking the money. We're hopeful we can recover it."

"Hopeful?"

"Beyond hopeful," Quinn said.

"Despite the cartel involvement?"

"Yes," I ventured.

"Regardless of the danger factor?"

"Yes."

"There's more?"

"Under the auspices of Special Agent Paul DeSavino, the FBI and the LAPD will raid two houses of ill repute, one located in West Hollywood and the other in Brentwood. Within the next hour or so."

"Houses of ill repute?"

"Cartel-run, top-drawer prostitution activities. Human trafficking. Involving illegals and underage women. They've been poised to launch this attack for some weeks. The raids, coupled with Quinn's cyber bust, are aimed at disrupting Los Perros and damaging its operations."

"I'm guessing there's even more."

"First thing tomorrow morning, the combined forces of the FBI and the San Diego Police Department will intercept a convoy of cartel-owned trucks, all containing significant amounts of heroin, oxycodone, morphine, and fentanyl."

"At the port?"

"Yes. We hope under the watchful gaze of Chuy Sanchez, the local kingpin."

"And Paulie wants to take him down?"

"He does."

"And where will you be?"

"George Town, Grand Cayman."

"Because?"

"That's where the money is."

"The stolen money?"

"Yes."

The Sheriff took a swig of the Beam. "This is all your doing, isn't it?"

"No."

"What no? It was you who instigated it, wasn't it?"

I stood. Quinn also stood.

"We have a plane to catch."

"I was right, you know."

"About?"

"You and the job."

"Not even close. I'll call you."

"This is good work, Buddy."

"Tell that to Quinn. She's the one who deserves the credit."

Quinn shrugged.

I hugged the old man, which embarrassed him.

Then Quinn and I headed for the county airport.

Once airborne in the Gulfstream III, a private jet the FBI had confiscated from a convicted Ponzi-schemer and loaned to us by Special Agent DeSavino's unit, we snacked on chicken Caesar salads and Argentinian wine, then settled in for the overnight flight.

There were four of us. In addition to Quinn and myself, we were carrying anesthesiologist Dr. David B. Muntz and Ashley Matthews, one of Quinn's computer geeks.

Matthews was with us to assist Quinn in her quest to capture the stolen money. Muntz was along for the prospect of our arresting and then extraditing Catalina Sanchez, who might prove to be uncooperative and in need of sedation.

Designed to accommodate upwards of seventeen passengers, this particular Gulfstream III had been reconfigured so that a portion of the cabin was a private bedroom.

The seats in the main cabin, similar to those in first class on commercial flights, also converted into flat beds.

Quinn Anthony immediately laid claim to the bedroom. She took my hand and led me in. "I've never done it on a plane," she whispered.

When I didn't say anything, she nuzzled my neck. "Come sleep with me, Buddy."

"No."

"I bet you've never done it on a plane."

"Once I did. On a transcon flight. With a flight attendant. In one of the lavs."

"Really?"

"Yeah. But we hit a stretch of turbulence and were knocked against the door. Which popped open and we tumbled into the aisle. I've never flown United since."

"You're such a jerk."

She pushed me out of the bedroom. "Who needs you?" She closed the door.

I converted my seat into a flat bed and slept soundly for nearly the full eight hours of flight time.

THIRTY-EIGHT

We arrived in George Town, the capital of the Cayman Islands as well as its financial hub, just after 10:00 a.m. local time.

We were met by FBI Special Agent Ginny Klebaur, who was stationed there. In her middle years and remarkably fit, Klebaur was a handsome woman, conservatively dressed, deeply tanned, and as serious as a heart attack.

"The van is fully equipped and parked inconspicuously in the strip mall lot," she said in a husky voice. "The two surveillance teams are in place. One in front, the other in back. Three teams. Eight-hour shifts. In case she shows up in the middle of the night."

She loaded us into a Chevy Tahoe and took us to the safe house located in the small residential district of George Town proper.

More opulent than I would have expected, the house contained four bedrooms and three baths. Ginny had arranged for a pair of FBI security officers to meet us upon our arrival. She insisted upon making certain we'd be protected twenty-four seven.

We dropped our bags, left Dr. Muntz at the house, and Quinn, Ashley, and I headed for the strip mall that was home to Rothberg & Sons Financial Services, Inc.

The mall also housed a Starbucks, a mini market, a liquor store, and a dry cleaner. Plus, it was across the road from the legendary Seven Mile Beach.

The van was elderly, dented, and in need of fresh paint. Inside was a different story. A banquette stacked with four Apple iMacs lined one of the walls, in front of which stood three ergonomically correct mesh desk chairs. Two straight-backed armchairs for the use of spectators were also available.

Quinn and Ashley immediately set about familiarizing themselves with the equipment and in short order had the Apples up and running.

Their focus was on establishing a link between their own algorithms and those of the Rothberg website. As Quinn had explained it, the link would allow them to breach Rothberg's web security and capture a split-second electronic snapshot of the moment when the data transitioned from Rothberg to the Catalina Sanchez protocols.

That snapshot would provide Quinn with all the information she'd require in order to invade the Sanchez site and siphon off its contents. Her algorithms were faster than Sanchez's, which would enable the theft.

"Now all we have to do is wait," Quinn said to me, mischief suddenly appearing in her eyes. "Care for a swim?"

"Excuse me?"

"We're in a holding pattern. On Grand Cayman island. Waiting for Catalina to show up. We've got deputies in place who will alert us when we're needed. And happily, we're steps away from one of the finest beaches in the Caribbean."

"You want to go to the beach?"

"I want to feel the sand between my toes."

"Okay."

"Okay what?"

"I'll go barefoot with you."

"I'll race you."

"Walking is good enough."

"Chicken," she chided and took off running.

I strolled across the road, stood gazing at the horizon for several moments, then took off my shoes and socks and walked toward the sea.

The beach was deserted. The tide was out, and gentle waves swept the shoreline where Quinn now stood, barefoot, relishing the warmth of the sea as it washed over her feet.

She looked at me. "I want to go in."

"In the water?"

"Yes."

"You have a bathing suit?"

She flashed a mischievous grin and started to remove her clothing.

"Hey," I chastised.

Too late. In no time she was naked and before she made tracks for the water, she handed me her clothes and without warning, wrapped her arms around me and kissed me. Then she stood back and assumed a provocative pose. "See anything you like?"

In an instant she was in the water, diving headfirst into the gentle surf, splashing and frolicking and gracefully swimming parallel to the shore.

I stood watching, hoping nothing untoward befell her. The beach remained empty. We were still the only people on this stretch.

She soon emerged, soaking wet.

"That was amazing," she stated unselfconsciously as she shook off the water.

Joyfully naked, she was truly beautiful. Her lithe body was agleam with reflected sunlight. I was distracted by an appreciation of her sensuousness. She moved closer to me, fully enjoying my discomfort.

She kissed me again, and to my dismay, I became aroused by her proximity, her nakedness, her scent, and the insistence of her tongue as it moistened my lips.

I stepped back.

She grinned.

Then, despite the fact she wasn't exactly dry, she wrestled

herself into her clothes, which clung to her suggestively. She knew full well the effect she was having on me, which made her giggle.

Then she took my hand and led me back to the strip mall.

THIRTY-NINE

The day proved uneventful. We were uncertain as to exactly when Catalina Sanchez would arrive in Grand Cayman. Or by what means.

Before Quinn sent Ashley Matthews away for several hours, she stopped by the safe house for a shower and a change of clothing. Then she took up her post in the communications van.

I met with FBI Special Agent Ginny Klebaur at a George Town café where, amid a gathering of sun-worshipping tourists, we reexamined our game plan.

"We'll know the moment she seeks entry to the island," Klebaur stated. "That is, if she does so legally."

"What entry wouldn't be legal?"

"Illicit entry by boat."

"Does that happen a lot?"

"It happens. But I'm not of a mind to believe she's prone to it."

"How will you know?"

"One way or the other, she has to show up at Rothberg Financial. There's no way she can access the funds otherwise."

"Because?"

"The funds are inexorably enmeshed with Quinn Anthony's algorithms. It was Catalina Sanchez herself who altered the security protocols that made it possible."

"She who lives by the sword…"

"Exactly."

"So?"

"Once the border patrol gets wind of her arrival, they'll so inform us and we'll deploy our agents."

"How many?"

"Eight."

"How quickly?"

"Quickly."

"The consequences?"

"Apprehension. And in Catalina's case, extradition."

"So what do we do?"

"We continue to wait."

We didn't have to wait much longer.

Following an uneventful evening, with Ashley Matthews and the rest of the security detail in place, Quinn and I retired to the safe house, allegedly for the night.

Although we had separate bedrooms, Quinn presented

herself at my door. "I'm not taking no for an answer," she averred
as she entered my room wearing only a see-through nightie.

My resolve was seriously shaken and when I didn't look
away, she became more emboldened. She shook off her nightie
and stood naked for several moments. "I know you want this as
much as I do."

I couldn't deny it.

It was just after she took off my shirt that my cell phone
began to shriek.

"Buddy Steel," I answered.

"She's here," Ginny Klebaur exclaimed. "Private jet. Accompanied by three security thugs."

"And?"

"I've deployed the team. We're stalling her at customs until
everyone's in place."

"Including me?"

"Especially you."

When I looked at her, Quinn's eyes were ablaze. "Boy, when
things go wrong..." she lamented and hurried off to get dressed.

As I watched her go, I realized I was suffering a deep sense of
disappointment.

Then I got over it.

FORTY

The black Mercedes limousine pulled to a stop directly in front of Rothberg Financial.

A burly man in a dark suit jumped out and scanned the area. He then assisted Catalina Sanchez from the back seat and escorted her into the Rothberg offices.

The limousine driver emerged, looked around, and with seemingly nothing else to do, he leaned against the driver's side door and began rummaging through the inside pocket of his dark suit jacket. At last he found what it was he was after. He removed the wrapper from a plastic toothpick and began working the left side of his mouth with it.

I watched this on the video monitors in the command vehicle. Hidden cameras provided bird's-eye views of the activities taking place both inside and outside the Rothberg offices.

My attention turned to Catalina Sanchez, who was not at all

what I expected. Tall and rangy, with an aristocratic air about her, she appeared to be in her early to mid-twenties. Stylishly dressed in a flowered, shoulderless Stella McCartney summer dress, her rich brown hair was wedge-cut, coyly framing her angular face with its Roman nose, Walter Keane–style large dark eyes, and her sultry, lipstick-free mouth.

I watched as a pompous-looking elderly gentleman in a bespoke white linen suit took hold of her hand and gently kissed it.

"What happens now?" I asked Quinn.

"She'll sign a bunch of papers. They'll reprogram the computer. The funds will move."

"To her personal account?"

"To where I direct it."

"How long?"

"How long what?"

"How long will it take?"

"You mean for the transfer?"

"Yes."

"I'll have it immediately."

"And when will she know she's been hacked?"

"Once the transfer's been made, she'll likely follow the normal protocol."

"Which is?"

"She'll make a big show of thanking the old man and use the computer to confirm receipt of the funds."

"And?"

"It will take her a few minutes to realize the dough has gone bye-bye. Then she'll go batshit."

Some years back I had been privileged to attend a one man show starring the legendary comedic magician Ricky Jay. In his act, Jay performed his signature illusion, Cards as Weapons.

With great flourish, Jay would place a normal playing card between his index and middle fingers, then fling it at top speed toward a chubby watermelon that sat stoically on a tall wooden stand.

Most of the time the card would penetrate the dense watermelon rind and adhere to it as proof that cards were as mighty as knives. But occasionally it didn't. The card would hit the watermelon, bounce off, and fall unceremoniously to the ground.

If this happened more than once during his act, Jay would surprise the audience by holding his right hand perpendicularly in front of himself and, with a shrug of his shoulders, a small pistol would miraculously appear in his hand as if from out of nowhere.

He would then point the gun at the watermelon and shoot it, all the while making snide remarks about how he didn't much care for that particular watermelon to begin with.

It was the surprise of seeing the gun magically appear in Ricky's hand that caught my attention.

The next day I visited a magic shop on Hollywood Boulevard and inquired as to where and how I might obtain a sling similar to Ricky Jay's.

When I explained that I wasn't a performer but was intrigued by how I might employ such a device as a law enforcement accessory, the proprietor suggested he might be able to make one for me.

After settling on a price, I provided him with a down payment and was told to return in a week.

Which I did.

The secret to the sling he produced was the strength of the thickened elastic that stretched tightly across the frame and was capable of being relaxed by a flick of the wrist. The force of the snapped elastic would propel the concealed weapon swiftly into the sling-wearer's hand. I spent many hours practicing the various idiosyncrasies of the sling-and-weapon combo, and in time, mastered it.

As predicted, Catalina completed the paperwork and we watched as the elderly gentleman pointed her to a Dell desktop into which she typed what appeared to be a series of numbers.

"Bingo," Quinn Anthony shouted.

There followed a moment of frantic activity as Quinn and Ashley programmed a plethora of data into their respective computers.

Then, after raptly studying a rapidly changing landscape of numbers and letters flashing across the computer screens, Quinn let out a rousing whoop. "We got it."

"You're sure?"

"Does a bear shit in the woods?" she admonished with a goofy grin.

I looked to Ginny Klebaur. "Shall we?"

She nodded.

As we had planned, and with a glance at Quinn Anthony, I hurriedly checked the Beretta Pico semi .380 that was secreted in the sling I had affixed to my forearm. Then I stepped out of the command vehicle and headed for the limousine.

The driver, still working his toothpick, took notice of me. Uncertain as to who I was and whether or not I might pose him a threat, he reached into his jacket pocket and produced a small Sig Sauer P320 handgun that he then held by his side.

I had on a loose-sleeved blue-and-white rugby shirt worn over a pair of khaki shorts. So as not to alarm the driver, I meandered...a local guy out for his afternoon constitutional.

The driver warily watched me and when I reached Rothberg Financial, I stopped and looked in the window. Then I stepped over to the front door.

The driver quickly approached me.

When I opened the front door, he banged into me and slammed it shut.

"Closed," he pronounced.

"But the door isn't locked."

"Closed," he repeated in a thick Hispanic accent.

"Look, whoever you are," I said, real friendly-like. "I'm a customer here and I've come to check on my holdings."

He gave me the once-over and again shook his head. Then he showed me his pistol.

His eyes widened when my own pistol magically appeared in my hand.

Without warning, I rammed my knee into his nuts and as he collapsed in sudden pain, I cold-cocked him with the Beretta. He fell to the ground and lay there motionless.

I grabbed the Sig Sauer and pocketed it. Then I cuffed his hands and tethered his legs, thereby disabling him.

I spotted Ginny Klebaur racing toward me, waving her arms. "Inside," she hollered.

Together, we entered Rothberg's. We passed through a small, empty waiting room and made our way down a narrow hallway that took us past a pair of unoccupied offices and led us to the one I recognized from the command vehicle monitors.

The scene inside was chaotic. The elderly man was seated at his desk, a look of confusion etched on his face.

A pair of FBI agents stood together, keeping a watchful eye on Catalina Sanchez and the other dark-suited bodyguard, who lay facedown on the floor, his hands cuffed behind him.

Sanchez was seated in one of the visitor's chairs across from the elderly man, also cuffed, her ankles bound together.

She radiated hostility, and when she spotted Ginny Klebaur, she started screaming. She stood, and despite her feet being bound, she lunged at Ginny, ferociously slashing her across the face with her cuffs.

Dr. David Muntz had slipped into the room. He held tight to a small medical kit bag. Ginny signaled to him. He extracted an already prepared hypodermic needle, stepped smartly to Catalina's side and administered the shot.

Catalina, reacting instinctively, tried to headbutt Muntz in the stomach, but almost immediately, the injected medicine took effect. She became visibly weakened and lost focus. Her oversized eyes grew glassy. Then she slumped to the floor, unconscious.

Dr. Muntz checked her. Then he stepped over to Ginny Klebaur, whose cheek had been bloodied by Sanchez. He produced a bottle of alcohol, some cotton swabs, and a bandage from his bag and proceeded to treat Klebaur's wound.

I asked Ginny to initiate the exit plan, and although unsettled by Sanchez's attack, she managed to voice the instruction.

I headed for the command vehicle to assist Quinn Anthony. She and Ashley had already dismantled and packed the computers and were ready to head for the airport. I told her what had occurred inside Rothberg Financial and inquired as to how she had fared.

"Far better than I imagined," she replied.

"Meaning?"

"We recovered all of the stolen money. All two-plus million of it."

"And?"

"The account contained in excess of sixty million."

"Sixty million dollars?"

"Sanchez must have been holding additional cartel swag. No wonder she went ballistic."

"Where's all of this so-called swag now?"

"Collecting dust in First Bank of San Remo."

"I'm guessing old man Sanchez must be one ruffled dude."

"Wow. A perceptive Gen Xer. Who could have imagined such a thing?"

FORTY-ONE

We had arranged to be driven to the airport in separate, inconspicuous vehicles. Ginny Klebaur would escort Catalina Sanchez and Dr. Muntz. Quinn and Ashley and their equipment were to be transported in a Nissan Rogue SUV.

In an effort to be as unassuming as possible, I rode in a local taxi.

Once at the airport, I checked in with Paul DeSavino.

"The shit's flying," he said when I finally got through to him.

"Is there perhaps an English translation of what you just said?"

"It would cost more."

"Paulie..."

"Yeah. Yeah. The house raids went off as planned. We hit both of them at the same time and were in and out before any kind of legal entanglement could occur."

"Again. English."

"No cartel lawyers gummed up the works. We liberated at least forty women who had been forced into sexual slavery. All management and security personnel were apprehended and turned over to ICE agents. We must have busted at least ten or so johns per venue. And we laid claim to each of the houses and confiscated their contents. Which, in one case, netted a weapons trove that looks to have been prepared for sale and subsequent transit out of the country."

"Sounds good."

"Better than good. The port raid was huge."

"How huge?"

"They're still inventorying the spoils, but one of my guys estimates a street value of over a hundred million."

"Excellent."

"And you?"

"Quinn Anthony says the account contained approximately sixty million."

"Wowee. We sure scorched their feathers."

"Did you get Chuy Sanchez?"

"Nah. He sniffed it out and split. Did you get the daughter?"

"Kicking and screaming."

"And you're taking her where?"

"I'll let you know when I get her there."

"He's compromised, Buddy. Not only did he lose close to two hundred million, but more importantly to him, his daughter is now in our custody. His fate is up for grabs."

"Meaning?"

"My money says he'll be MIA in no time."

"You mean the cartel will take him out?"

"I mean he'll go to ground before that happens. If he senses he's a marked man, he'll split."

"Leaving the daughter behind?"

"His worst nightmare."

"Resolvable?"

"Who knows? But I'm hoping not in the usual way."

"Meaning?"

"I'm going to make a recommendation to you, Buddy. Don't dismiss it out of hand."

"What?"

"I think you should vanish for a while."

"Because?"

"He doesn't know about me or about Quinn or about anyone other than you involved in orchestrating his downfall. You can be sure he's pissed. And with no one else to blame, I'm surmising he's gonna come for you with guns blazing."

We were aboard the Gulfstream III.

Dr. Muntz and Catalina Sanchez were in the bedroom, she sedated, he preparing to feign sleep when the time came.

Ashley Matthews was in the lavatory. The door was closed but unlocked. The green light was on, indicating the room was empty, when in fact, it wasn't.

Quinn and I were in the main cabin, seated across from each other.

Ginny Klebaur was escorting a customs official through the plane in preparation for our departure. I was fairly certain that the official was owned and operated by the FBI.

I watched as Quinn knocked on the bedroom door and then opened it a crack so the official could have a look inside.

The plan was to persuade customs that the sleeping Catalina Sanchez was Ashley Matthews. Ashley, stashed in the john, would escape detection because it was Ginny's plan to hustle the customs officer off the plane without him looking into the tiny WC.

"Ms. Matthews is asleep," Quinn said to the official. "She had a rather exhausting jaunt through the various George Town casinos and her husband, Dr. Muntz, who accompanied her, is barely awake himself."

I could hear Dr. Muntz grunting his agreement.

"Is there some photo ID of Ms. Matthews I might have a look at?"

Having anticipated the official would demand at least some form of ID, Ginny had borrowed Ashley's passport, inserted a prepared photo of Catalina and, in turn, briefly flashed it in front of the official.

Barely glancing at it, he returned the passport to Ginny, who guided him away from the restroom and into the main cabin where Quinn and I presented our passports.

Satisfied we were legit, the customs officer allowed Ginny to escort him from the plane.

After several minutes, she returned. "You're cleared to go," she said to me.

"Great work, Ginny. Thanks."

She smiled. "I'll do my best to keep you out of it, Buddy. But despite the video-recorded evidence of your having acted in self-defense, it's possible you may have to testify."

"Let me know."

She looked at Quinn and then back at me. She flashed us both a thumbs-up and exited the plane.

FORTY-TWO

When I finally arrived at the office, Marsha Russo was all over me, brandishing a stack of phone messages. "Seems like everybody in San Remo wants a piece of you."

"All that's left are remnants."

"Jordyn Yates is at the top of the list."

I dialed Jordyn as Marsha left the office.

"Forgive my French," she said, "but where in the fuck were you?"

"Special assignment."

"On Grand Cayman?"

"Some people have all the luck. What's up, Jordy?"

"Jeffrey Brice has vanished."

"What?"

"His father claims he skipped."

"He skipped bail?"

"His old man said something riled him."

"What?"

"Something to do with Jill."

"What was it?"

"You picked her up."

"So?"

"The old man said Jeffrey freaked."

"Because I picked her up?"

"That's what he said. I think we need to talk, Buddy. In person."

"Your place or mine?"

"Halfway."

"I'll make the reservation."

We met at the Malibu Beach Inn, a luxury oceanfront hotel on Pacific Coast Highway. Dinner was in the hotel dining room. I was already seated when Jordyn arrived.

I watched as she stood in the doorway, scanning the room. She was stunning in a black, scoop-necked, Fabiana Pigna summer frock. A joyful smile that emphasized her prominent cheekbones and sensuous lips lit up her face when she spotted me.

I stood to greet her and we shared a hug. She leaned back and gave me her infamous once-over. "You look like you could use some sleep."

"Tell me about it."

"What's going on in Buddy world?" she inquired as we sat.

A bottle of her favorite prosecco was chilling in an ice bucket beside the table, and a server raced over to pour her a glass. She smiled and thanked him, then downed a healthy swig. He refilled the glass before heading off.

"I'm making the world safe from cybercrime."

"Any fun?"

"None I can detect. It's a strange new world out there."

"One day you'll tell me about it."

"One day I hope I'll understand it."

She smiled. "Jill Nelson?"

"Safe."

"Where?"

"South San Remo."

"What have you learned?"

"She says Jeffrey Brice is out to kill her."

"Because?"

"She claims he lied. It was he who masterminded the whole thing. Not her. And with her out of the picture, there's no one who can pin it on him."

"So he wants to kill her?"

"That's what she claims."

"What do you think?"

"It doesn't matter what I think. I'm ready to turn the whole thing over to the DA and wash my hands of it."

She sipped more prosecco. "We still have the matter of the Brice lawsuit."

"Even though Jeff's disappeared?"

"It's not a winning ploy, that's for sure."

"So?"

"With your permission, I'd like to petition the court to vacate the suit."

"Permission granted."

"Next case."

"Meaning?"

"Jill Nelson's father is threatening to sue you."

"Excuse me?"

"Claims you're unlawfully holding his daughter."

"She's terrified she's going to be murdered."

"The father doesn't believe it."

"So what do you advise?"

"Release her to the custody of the father."

"And if the currently missing Jeffrey Brice kills her?"

"Good question. I'll talk to the DA."

I nodded.

"I presume you'll want to retain my services regarding the possible Nelson lawsuit."

"Excellent presumption."

"And terminate my services regarding the Jeffrey Brice lawsuit."

"If you succeed in having the case thrown out."

"Dinner?"

"Absolutely."

I signaled the server, who made tracks to the table

brandishing a pair of menus. He refilled Jordyn's glass, then stood self-consciously awaiting our orders. When we finally decided, he scribbled them down and scurried away.

"Who is she?" Jordyn asked.

"Excuse me?"

"Why have you been avoiding me?"

"I haven't been avoiding you. I told you, I've been wrapped up in this cybercrime business."

"You don't fool me, Buddy. My instincts tell me there's someone else."

"It's nothing. Nothing's happened."

"So there is someone."

"It's not what you think."

"Well, if nothing's happened, it suggests that something might have happened or is still in the throes of possibly happening."

"Lawyers," I muttered.

"Who is she?"

"She's a millennial with an unsteady grip on reality."

"Oh. my."

"Exactly. She's a technology geek who runs her own company. She's been instrumental in solving our series of cyber thefts. She's exactly what you might expect. Sharp as a tack. Warily self-confident. Insufferably arrogant and a charter member of the no-commitment aristocracy."

"The girl of your dreams."

"She's made every effort to bed me."

"Is she worth bedding?"

"I wouldn't know. But she's very attractive."

"And you're torn."

"Don't ask me why."

"And me?"

"The reverse."

"Meaning?"

"My turn in the noncommitment barrel."

"Maybe therapy isn't such a bad idea for you, Buddy."

"I'm on overwhelm just now. I'm back here against my better instincts. Trying to make sense of these cybercrimes. My old man is no help. Plus, he's decided to retire and wants to name me his successor. I can't remember my last good night's sleep. I feel like I'm fraying at the seams."

"So I guess suggesting we skip dessert and go rip our clothes off isn't exactly the best idea."

"It might not be."

"Do you think there's a chance you might actually grow up someday, Buddy?"

"Lately, I haven't been too optimistic about it."

"I can't imagine why."

FORTY-THREE

It was 2:30, and the freeway was empty. We had decided not to use the hotel room, and I was on my way home when the phone rang.

"It's 2:30 in the morning."

"And what? You were sleeping?" Quinn Anthony exclaimed.

"I'm driving."

"At 2:30 in the morning? What are you, nuts? People your age shouldn't be allowed to drive at 2:30 in the morning. Especially you."

"Why have you called, Quinn?"

"It's in bitcoins."

"What is?"

"The sixty million. Plus, it shot up in value. It's now worth seventy million."

"How could that be?"

"Do you know anything about cyber currency?"

"Just tell me, will you please?"

"It changes in value."

"What does that mean?"

"It's a fluctuating market. It could go up or down at a moment's notice."

"So why don't you grab the extra ten million and run?"

"I already did."

"How?"

"I converted the bitcoins into dollars. Seventy million of them."

"So this is all good news."

"You know what I find interesting about you, Buddy?"

"What?"

"How you somehow manage to get all kinds of people to do all kinds of things for you."

When I didn't respond, she went on. "Which is pretty astonishing considering what a jerk you are."

"That's a very kind thing to say."

"I thought so."

After a lengthy silence, I asked, "Was there anything else?"

"When can I see you, Buddy? I'm still reeling from what went down in the Caymans."

"I don't know."

"What don't you know?"

"The *what happens after* part."

"What if I said I'd move in with you? Make a commitment."

"I wouldn't believe you."

"Why not?"

"Because millennials don't understand the concept."

"A lot of us do."

"But you're not one of them."

"You think?"

"I know."

I knew something was wrong the minute I parked my Wrangler. The hair on the back of my neck was standing at attention.

I slipped out of the car just as the windshield exploded. Shattered glass flew everywhere. The bullet embedded itself into the driver's seat.

I ducked down beside the car, grabbed my Colt Combat Commander and quickly press-checked it.

I had parked in front of the row of hedges that separated my apartment building from the parking lot. I glanced at the hedges but saw nothing.

Another shot buzzed past my ear and again I hit the dirt.

When I looked up, I detected movement from behind one of the hedges. I fired at it and was met in return by a hail of bullets.

I could barely make out the shape of the man, now moving swiftly away.

I raced toward the hedges and ducked through them just in time to see the shooter round a corner of the building.

I followed.

When I reached the corner, I crept into a space between hedges and waited.

It wasn't long before I heard movement and, a moment later, saw the man peek around the corner.

My shot caught him in the side, and yowling, he dropped to the ground.

I leapt from the hedges and found the man lying on the ground, grasping his side, his pistol beside him. I picked it up, removed the cartridge, and then threw it away.

I stood over the man who was doing his best to stanch the blood that was leaking from the wound in his side.

He appeared to be in his mid- to late twenties. Frightened. Confused. He looked at me pleadingly.

"Take off your shirt," I instructed. "Hold it against the wound."

He gingerly did so.

"Who are you?"

He said nothing.

"You have a choice. You either tell me who you are and I phone for an ambulance. Or you say nothing and I watch you bleed out."

"Sanchez," he murmured.

"What Sanchez?"

"Chuy Sanchez. I work for him. He made me do this."

I yanked out my cell phone and called the station. The new guy, Mickey Alpert, answered. "It's Buddy. I need an ambulance at my building. A downed assailant. Shot in the side. ASAP."

"Copy that," Alpert said.

I turned my attention to the downed assailant.

"Will I die?" he whimpered.

"You will. But likely not today. EMTs are on their way."

"I have no personal beef with you," the assailant said.

I nodded.

"It was either kill or be killed."

I nodded again.

"I'm sorry I ever came to this country."

"Not to worry. You'll be back home in no time."

I heard the siren of the approaching ambulance. I watched it round the bend, pull into the lot, and screech to a stop behind my car.

A pair of paramedics exited, spotted me, and headed in my direction.

"How bad?" the first medic asked.

"He'll live."

While the first medic examined the fallen gunman, the second removed a stretcher from the back of the ambulance and hurried toward us. Together, the medics loaded the wounded man onto it.

"A police officer will meet you at Freedom General. He'll keep watch."

The driver nodded his assent and sped off.

I phoned Mickey Alpert and instructed him to contact the Freedom police and have them dispatch an officer to the hospital.

Finally, I headed inside.

It was 4:00 a.m., and although I was sleep-deprived, I didn't figure myself a candidate for any during what little remained of the night.

I debated as to whether or not I should call Quinn and ask her to come rock me gently to dreamland.

Then I thought better of it.

FORTY-FOUR

It was Chanho Pineda who startled me awake at 6:30. "What?"
I mumbled.

"Why do you sound so awful?"

"It's a long story. What's up?"

"I heard you had a visitor."

"Compliments of Chuy Sanchez."

"Who's about to become toast. The supreme commander has
had enough of him. Word is he's pulling the plug."

"Which means?"

"Within a matter of days Los Perros will have new leadership."

"How will that affect what's going on?"

"Cosmetically speaking, it will put a new face on an old dog.
Realistically, everything will likely remain the same, but the
methodology might undergo renovation."

"Why?"

"The Salvadorians have close to two hundred million reasons why. They withstood the Sanchez idiosyncrasies so long as the money poured in. But the raids put a serious dent in that reality. The cybercrimes failure was greeted poorly by the cartel bosses, who are essentially a group of ancients whose comprehension of the ways and means of the new technologies is pitiful.

"They have adopted a new philosophy. *If it ain't broke, don't fix it.* Thus, *adios* Chuy Sanchez. *Buenos dias* to new leadership of old philosophies."

"And you're telling me this because?"

"It may take a few days for it to play itself out. In the meantime, it's known that Señor Sanchez is hot to eliminate you. He blames you for pretty much everything."

"So?"

"You need to lay low for a spell. Get lost. Disappear."

"And if I don't?"

"Don't tempt fate, Buddy. Sanchez has become irrelevant. It's a good guess he knows it. He's likely making his own plans to vanish. But it's a sure bet his last remaining piece of unfinished business is you. Listen to me, Buddy. Get out of Dodge."

"I don't like the optics."

"Fuck the optics."

"What kind of time frame are we talking about?"

"Anywhere from days to weeks."

"And when the makeover occurs?"

"Sanchez is a pariah. He's a dead man walking. And the new leadership will be too involved in the takeover to worry about any grudges he held. Just do it, Buddy. It won't be for long. Hit the mattresses. Lay low. I'll let you know when it's safe to emerge."

"Another tough call," I mused.

I weighed my options. I could hit the mattresses, as Chanho suggested. Or I could brazen it out. Surround myself with bodyguards and await word that Chuy has been neutralized.

I asked myself what would be in the best interests of the Sheriff's Department?

I invited ADA Skip Wilder to stop by for a coffee on his way to the office. We had been friends since junior high. I knew he'd provide an unprejudiced overview and recommend a reasonable solution.

"What do you think I should do?"

"Find a new line of work," he chided as he polished off one of the two chocolate crullers he had brought with him. We were sitting at my kitchen table on this, a rainy morning, the inherent gloom of which had already infected me.

"Do you think you could be a little more helpful, Skip?"

"What worries you the most?"

"The image of a sheriff running scared."

"So, don't run scared."

"And do what?"

"Stay visible, all the while being invisible."

"How do I accomplish that?"

"Camouflage."

"Meaning?"

"You vacate the apartment while at the same time you post guards around the building so as to mislead any of the bozos who might come calling. Let them think you're holed up inside."

"When all the time I'm somewhere else."

"Hiding out."

"That's a good idea, Skip."

"So can I go to work now?"

I smiled.

"Let me ask you a question," he said.

"Go on."

"You going to eat that cruller?"

I consulted Marsha Russo.

Without hesitation she organized a team of deputies and local police officers who would stand guard at my building in shifts, the first group of which would show up within the hour.

I packed a bag with the stuff I would need for a short sojourn.

I surmised it would benefit the office if I didn't actually leave town. I'd likely be noticed were I to suddenly appear elsewhere.

As Skip suggested, I needed a place in San Remo County where I could safely hunker down. Where I could be visible were it necessary. And invisible the rest of the time.

I chalk up the decision I made in large part to sleep-deprivation.

But in reality, I knew damn well how neurotic it was.

FORTY-FIVE

Under cover of the rain, disguised in an oversized trench coat, horn-rimmed glasses, floppy hat, and the Groucho Marx mustache she brought for me, I was spirited away from my apartment by Marsha Russo.

As a trio of officers stirred up a commotion at the front of the building, we fled through a side door adjacent to which her car was parked.

During a leisurely tour of the winding and twisting side streets of Freedom, Marsha made certain we weren't being followed. When she was satisfied, she picked up the pace and made tracks for San Remo.

"May I render my opinion?" she ventured.

"Have I a choice?"

"You know I've always loved and respected you, Buddy. And I admire how highly skilled you are. Light years ahead of the pack."

She gazed briefly away from the road and flashed me a miniaturized version of her "look."

"I'm betting there's a qualification coming, isn't there?"

"This is easily the nuttiest thing I've ever seen you do."

"Thank you."

"It wasn't a compliment."

"May I offer a quote from one of the world's great philosophers?"

"Must you?"

"In the immortal words of Socrates himself, *Mind your own fucking business.*"

"You're sure you don't want security?" Marsha asked when she dropped me in front of the house.

"Positive."

"You'll stay in regular contact."

"As promised."

"The San Remo police are on alert and will respond immediately if needs be."

I smiled, grabbed my bag, and got out of the car.

Marsha lowered the window. "It's not too late to change your mind."

Without responding, I headed for the door, which opened before I got there. Once I was inside, Quinn Anthony closed it behind me. She was standing in front of me, wearing a blue-and-white unbuttoned pajama top and nothing else. A sly grin illuminated her face.

"In case you're wondering, I gave the staff the week off. Told them I had the flu," she explained as she put her arms around my neck and leaned into me. "I can't hardly believe this, Buddy."

She kissed me. Looked into my eyes and kissed me again. "You know what I want?"

When I didn't answer, she went on. "I want you to fuck my brains out is what I want."

"Wow. What about the foreplay?"

"That was the foreplay."

She was right about one thing. The sex was terrific. She was agile and inventive, brazen as well as demure, but as I soon came to realize, while her lovemaking was dexterous and dizzying, it was emotionally vapid.

At one juncture, following a particularly exhaustive joust, as we were mellowing in our afterglow, I asked, "How do you feel?"

"A little sore."

"No. Not that. How do you feel about us?"

"About us? What do you mean 'about us'?"

"I don't know, Quinn. We've opened ourselves up to each other in a very powerful manner. Unguarded. Uninhibited. It's clearly impacted me. I feel emotionally vulnerable in a way I haven't before."

"What is it you're saying, Buddy?"

"I guess I'm saying I have feelings for you. Feelings heightened by the intensity of our lovemaking."

Instinctively, she shied away. "I don't know what to say. I mean I'm having a swell time and all. I really like being with you. But I'm not connecting the emotional dots."

"Meaning?"

"I always said I emulated you. What was your mantra? *I'd rather hook up than settle down.'* That's my mantra, too, Buddy. That's exactly how I feel."

After that, things changed.

I had put my emotions on the line and expressed my feelings. Which left her dumbfounded and me wounded. And, surprisingly, hurt.

The view from the other side of the street. Which I'd never experienced before.

What was it Jordyn asked? Was I ever planning to grow up? That question now sneaked into my consciousness.

The pace and intensity of our lovemaking slowed. Quinn went about her life, seemingly oblivious to my emotional withdrawal.

She was a slave to her cell phone. And although she never actually answered it, it chimed incessantly, each obnoxious chime indicating the arrival of either a new email or text message. She was distracted by it every time.

She continuously played what she referred to as *her music,* a mixed bag of discordant, indecipherable, monosyllabic noise.

It drove me crazy.

I discovered it wasn't so much the cultural protocols that marked our differences, it was the technological ones that had the biggest impact. She was glued to the social media outlets. Widely connected to an illusory universe. Immediately responsive to a galaxy of alleged *friends.*

But despite her so-called tuned-in existence, she was essentially isolated. Although I knew her to be a skilled and talented collaborator, in her private life she was a loner, digitally connected, yet oddly adrift.

It occurred to me that Marsha was right. This *was* possibly the nuttiest thing I had ever done.

But on the other hand, lessons learned the hard way are lessons well learned.

I phoned Jordyn Yates from the privacy of a bathroom. She agreed without hesitation.

Marsha was there in less than an hour, an hour during which I packed my few belongings and sat Quinn down to tell her I was leaving.

"I knew this wouldn't work," she said.

"But you didn't say anything."

"Because I wasn't exactly sure."

"You're a very special person, Quinn. These few days with you have taught me a great deal."

"Like what? Don't get mixed up with a millennial?"

"Something more psychologically relevant."

"Such as?"

"Something personal."

"So you're dumping me is what you're saying."

"I don't interpret it that way."

"In what way do you interpret it?"

"I see it as a rite of passage."

"More Gen X bullshit."

"It is if you think it is."

"I know it is."

Marsha had packed a new bag for me, and I was soon on my way to Jordyn's cabin in Deer Valley, Utah.

I felt as if a great weight had been lifted. I saw my life in a different light. I had been forced to come to grips with the psychological underpinnings that guided me into a willing participation in a conspiracy to do myself harm. Analytically speaking, of course.

My mind was filled with the new realization of who and what I am. And how I might take steps to right my emotional wrongs.

Very heady stuff.

Heady enough to have distracted me from checking the underside of the Wrangler in search of any tracking devices that might have been placed there.

Which allowed a silver Prius Hatchback to craftily track me all the way to Utah without revealing its presence.

FORTY-SIX

Jordy's cabin was located steps from the vaunted Deer Valley ski run, on a mountainside bordered by a vast forest. It was her sanctuary, a refuge from the rough-and-tumble world of her myriad legal challenges.

Constructed of rough-hewn logs and mortar, it reflected her eclectic aesthetics. Thick, colorful Indian rugs blanketed redwood plank floors. Sofas and overstuffed armchairs fronted a brick-lined fireplace in the living/dining area. The kitchen was newly modernized. A whirlpool tub and shower combo took up the better part of the bathroom.

I dropped my bag on the queen-sized bed, put away the groceries I had picked up at the market at the foot of the hill, and with a fair amount of daylight remaining, dressed for a late afternoon hike.

I strapped on my boots and adjusted my kit belt, then exited the back door, made my way through a tiny changing hut, and stepped out onto the run.

The first thing I noticed was the red-tailed hawk that had planted itself on a branch of the aspen tree that faced the cottage. Colorful and regal, the hawk was swaying with the intermittent wind and appeared to be enjoying the ride.

The second thing I noticed was a tough-looking lout, dressed in black, emerging from the surrounding woods, holding a Smith & Wesson nine-millimeter Shield handgun that was pointed at me.

"Hands where I can see them," the thug said in a pronounced Hispanic accent.

I stood rooted to the spot, my hands in front of me.

The man approached and, with his pistol pressed to my temple, proceeded to pat me down in search of any weapons. Satisfied I was clean, he stepped back and pointed to my kit belt. "Take it off and toss it here."

I did as he instructed.

"*Está bueno*," he called out.

I watched as Chuy Sanchez stepped out of the woods. He looked at his associate, who nodded. Then he approached me.

Without warning, he slapped me in the face. "You couldn't just leave it alone, could you?" he spit out. "You had to go and fuck it all up."

He slapped me again, this time bloodying my lip. "The time has come for you to be held to account."

He nodded to his associate, who took several steps in my direction, raising his Smith & Wesson as he did so.

"You're about to learn the true meaning of suffering, Mr.

Steel. Just so you have an idea of what your final moments will bring, Señor Guzman here is well-practiced in the art of torture," Chuy taunted.

He suddenly wound up and punched me in the stomach. I dropped to my knees, gasping for breath.

He yanked me to my feet.

"First your arms. Then your legs. And when you're no longer able to stand, he's going to joyfully use you as a trampoline."

Sanchez stepped back and turned to Señor Guzman. "Make him suffer."

Snickering, Señor Guzman took a step in my direction, but he barely had time to acknowledge the Berreta Pico pistol that had magically appeared in my hand before I shot him center mass.

Confusion reigned in Chuy Sanchez's eyes as he watched his henchman collapse. He turned to me, the realization of what had just occurred beginning to dawn on him.

"You son of a bitch," he said.

Clumsily, he made a move for what I took to be a weapon secreted in one of his jacket pockets. After years of being surrounded by armed protectors, it appeared as if he had grown unaccustomed to defending himself.

I turned the Beretta toward him. "I wouldn't if I were you."

"You would if you were staring at my fate," he said as he produced a Walther P22 semi and turned it in my direction. "I'm already dead."

"It ain't over 'til it's over."

"What's that? Some kind of cheap philosophy? How stupid

do you think I am, Steel? You won. I lost. Just do a dead man a favor, will you?"

I said nothing. He glared at me. "Do you have children, Mr. Steel?"

"No."

"Have you any sense of the emotional bond between a father and daughter?"

I shrugged.

"It's the most significant relationship you can have. You should have cut my daughter some slack, Mr. Steel," he said as he raised his pistol.

I killed him before he could get off the shot.

––––––––––––

I pondered these events. Not only had I killed two men, but one of them was a cartel bigwig who as much as committed suicide by cop.

I asked myself why.

"Because there was already a rumored reward being offered for any gang member who offed him," I answered. "The Feds were hot on his trail. I surmised he didn't have much taste for life on the run or in prison. And having come face-to-face with that reality, he sought revenge on me by goading me into implementing his preconceived exit strategy."

I set about concealing the two bodies in the nearby forest. I wasn't certain exactly what to do, but I knew that were the two bodies discovered where they fell, it might place an inexorable stain on Jordyn's cabin. One she could never remove.

So, brandishing the set of keys I found in Chuy's pocket, I set off in search of his car.

I wandered out onto the roadway, where I soon located the Prius, stashed in a short stretch of undeveloped land, partially camouflaged by wild brush and tall grasses.

Darkness was falling when I backed it into Jordyn's driveway.

I popped the trunk and, although it was a struggle, I managed to drag each of the bodies to the car and then, with no small degree of difficulty, hoist them into the trunk.

I removed their wallets and whatever else might identify them. Then I closed the trunk and smeared the car's exterior and both license plates with enough mud to distort them.

I was intent upon moving the Prius to a place where it couldn't be traced in any way to Jordyn Yates. A place where the two deaths wouldn't be connected to me.

McCarran International, the Las Vegas airport, located equidistant between Deer Valley and Los Angeles, appeared to be my best option.

Once off the mountain, despite it being just after eleven p.m., I phoned her.

She answered sleepily. "What could you possibly want at this hour?"

"Do you have a burner phone?"

"Somewhere, I do."

"Find it and call me back."

Several minutes later my cell phone rang.

"I need you to meet me in Vegas. In front of Treasure Island. Five a.m."

I ended the call without waiting for a response. I didn't want anything regarding this matter memorialized in any phone records.

FORTY-SEVEN

It was nearing 4:30 when I pulled off the I-15 and made a brief stop. I donned the trench coat, floppy hat, and horn-rimmed sunglasses Marsha had earlier provided, as well as the Groucho mustache I had altered so it no longer looked comical. Then I headed for McCarran Airport Terminal 3.

Once a sleepy venue, as Las Vegas matured so had the airport. Host to dozens of international airlines, the terminals now mirrored the garish Vegas glitz. Banks of gaudy slot machines loudly greet new arrivals and, in turn, offer one final frolic with Lady Luck to those on their way home.

I knew I would be photographed when I entered the long-term parking lot, so in addition to the disguise, I made a point of looking away from the camera as the machine disgorged my ticket. Then I quickly drove away.

In the anonymity of the myriad rows of parked cars, I sprayed bleach over the interior of the Prius so as to remove all traces of myself. Then I locked it up and made tracks for the terminal.

I smudged any prints that might have remained on the car keys with my shirttail, then tossed them into one of the parking lot dumpsters.

Still in disguise, I hurried through the terminal and grabbed the first cab in line.

"The Mirage," I instructed.

I opened the newspaper I had purchased inside and lowered my head as if to read it, thereby shielding my face so it wasn't visible in the rearview mirror.

"That'll be ten fifty," the driver said as he pulled up in front of the Mirage hotel.

Without making eye contact, I handed him three fives, thanked him, and got out of the cab.

Instead of entering the hotel, however, I walked toward Las Vegas Boulevard, where I made a left turn and headed up the street to Treasure Island.

Even at this early hour there were numbers of pedestrians on the boulevard, enjoying the cool weather and the less frenetic crowds.

As I strolled, I surreptitiously slipped out of my trench coat, removed the floppy hat, and placed them both inside my shoulder bag.

By the time I reached the Treasure Island Pirate Ship display, I had also removed the mustache and swapped my sunglasses for a pair of horn-rimmed eyeglasses.

When I jumped into Jordyn's Lexus hybrid, I bore little or no resemblance to the person from the long-term parking lot.

If a photographic trail existed, one spliced together from the many cameras posted almost everywhere along my route, establishing a positive identification would be daunting.

"Dare I ask where we're going?" Jordyn asked once I was settled.

"Deer Valley."

She followed the signs to the I-15 and within minutes we were heading north.

"Is there any chance you might tell me what in God's name is going on?"

"Only if you ask nicely."

"I'm in no mood, Buddy..."

I explained what happened.

"Wow."

"Exactly."

"So there's no trace of it at the cottage?"

"None."

"And no one saw you?"

"It was late. The road was empty. Not a single car between the cottage and the 15."

"So what happens to them?"

"Sooner or later."

"Sooner or later what?"

"Someone's going to get hip to what smells so bad in the parking lot."

"Not to mention the car will have been there for a spell."

"Long-term parking. It'd be at least a couple of weeks before security became suspicious."

"So you think the smell will give it away."

"I do."

It was about half an hour later when she said, "You're certain no one can trace the Prius to the cottage?"

"I am."

"What about your disguise? The possessions you lifted from them? Stuff like that?"

"They're in my bag."

"And?"

"Fire."

"What fire?"

"Fireplace fire. I intend to turn everything into cinders."

"When?"

"As soon as we get to the cottage."

"And then?"

"Sleep."

"You're going to sleep while all this stuff is burning?"

"Only if it's okay with you."

"Why wouldn't it be okay with me?"

"I don't know. Is it okay?"

"Why are you acting like such a creep?"

She took her eyes off the road for a moment and looked at me.

I met her gaze. "Are you angry with me, Jordy?"

"Why would I be angry with you?"

I shrugged. "I don't know. Maybe because of my indiscretion."

"What indiscretion?"

"What we discussed the last time we spoke."

"Oh, now I get it."

"Get what?"

"You feel guilty about it, don't you?"

I shrugged.

"You have nothing to be ashamed of, Buddy. Whatever happened, if anything, has nothing to do with me. Any perceived indiscretion is in your head. Not mine."

"Seriously?"

"Of course seriously. We're friends, you and I. We're not married. We're not even a couple. We're friends."

"With no strings?"

"None."

"And you're not pissed at me because of what happened at the cottage?"

"You had no choice. And you endangered yourself so as to protect me. To my way of thinking, that was admirable."

"You think?"

"Those were bad guys, Buddy. Really bad guys who did really bad things. Plus, you acted in self-defense. And the world's a safer place for it."

After that we drove pretty much in silence. As the roadway widened and we sped through a lengthy stretch of empty land, I found myself dozing, only to be jostled awake when she made the turn onto Deer Valley Road. It was close to nine a.m. when we pulled into her driveway.

Awake but groggy, I accompanied her inside.

With the help of some old newspapers, I lit a fire. Once it was ablaze, I tossed the contents of my bag onto it. I watched as the stuff ignited and burned.

"Hungry?" Jordyn asked.

"Sleepy."

She pointed me toward the bedroom.

I smiled weakly. "Just a short nap."

I slept until my cell phone began chirping. Which was about an hour later.

FORTY-EIGHT

"She killed a police officer and escaped," Marsha Russo announced.

"Who did?"

"Jill Nelson."

"She killed an officer?"

"I just got a call from the East Freedom Police Station. Captain Andrew MacLeod. He told me. Officers Manuel Romero and Jack Rose were on duty. A couple of hours ago. They hear a cry for help coming from the cell block. Jill Nelson is the sole occupant. Romero goes to see what's happening.

"According to Rose, Romero finds Jill lying on the floor of her cell, in a fetal position, moaning. He tells Rose about it when he comes to fetch the cell key. Then he goes back to the cell.

"The next thing Rose hears is a gunshot.

"Alarmed, he reaches for his sidearm just as Jill bursts through the cell block door. She suddenly spots Rose and fires at him. He hits the deck. She exits the jailhouse. Instead of chasing her, he goes to see what's happened to Romero, who he finds dead on the floor of her cell. He then heads outside in search of Jill. She's gone. As is Romero's personal vehicle. A Ford pickup."

"Jesus."

"Captain MacLeod is beside himself dealing with Romero's death. What should I do, Buddy?"

"This doesn't make a whole lot of sense. I mean, why would she do it?"

"Should I put it on the wire?"

"I suppose so. Armed and dangerous."

"If she's out there on her own," Marsha said, "doesn't she have a Jeffrey Brice issue?"

"He wants to kill her, you mean."

"That's what I thought. You believe this could have something to do with Jeffrey Brice?"

"It's a puzzlement. That's for sure. Look, I'll be back tomorrow. I'll head out first thing in the morning."

"You're coming back here tomorrow?"

"Yes."

"What about Chuy Sanchez?"

"What about him?"

"He'll know you're here."

"Are the troops still posted at my place?"

"Yes."

"Then I'll take my chances," I said and ended the call.

We both had a hankering for beef, so we ventured down to Ruth's Chris in Park City for a steak and martini dinner. After which we strolled around town, marveling at how it had grown and changed.

Still weary from our respective journeys, we decided to call it an early night.

"I'll be happy to sleep on the sofa," I said to her as we readied ourselves for bed.

"No need."

"Will it be awkward?"

"What? Sleeping in the same bed with you?"

I nodded.

"We've been down this road before. It won't be awkward in the least. And who knows, it might even render a surprise or two," she said with a wink.

The surprise came sometime during the night, when I climbed back into bed following a bathroom visit.

Jordyn had stirred and once I was settled, she repositioned herself so that in effect we were spooning. Her proximity had its effect. Before long we were embracing, and then one thing led to another.

Our ease with each other was comfortable, tender, and loving. I think we were both surprised by how connected we felt.

Although I left in the early morning, Jordy stayed, safe in her sanctuary, content to have an unexpected couple of days alone and quiet.

I was nearing Zion when she called. "May I tell you something?"

"Please."

"We're good together, you and I."

"We are."

"Whatever it is we share, it's meaningful."

"For me, too."

"We go back a ways."

"We do."

"And we always seem to get better."

"We do."

"So what do you think?"

"About what?"

"Commitment."

"I don't really know, Jordy. But I agree with everything you said."

"What if we behaved as if we were a pair of grown-ups."

"Meaning?"

"What if we pledged ourselves to each other."

"You mean you want to get married?"

"God, no. I mean what if we were to commit to spending time together. Regular time. Planned. Not haphazard. You know, what if we behaved like we were a couple?"

"Would you want to do that?"

"Would you?"

"I suppose we're not getting any younger," I mused.

"Should I interpret that inanity as a yes?"

"You could. What about you?"

After a short silence, she said, "Let me get this straight, Buddy. You're agreeing we should now consider ourselves a couple?"

"I think so."

"So you understand what you just agreed to?"

"Quit being so condescending. Yes, I understand."

"Well, I'll be damned."

"Me, too."

FORTY-NINE

I met up with FBI Special Agent Paul DeSavino as planned at the
ICE Detention Center in the city of Oceanside, a vast spread of
warehouses, once home to a seafood processing company that
had gone belly-up.

Three of the warehouses had been converted into holding
cells and the property secured by electrically charged fencing.
And despite any number of attempts to disinfect it, the thousands of detainees who passed through on a daily basis still
complained it reeked of fish.

DeSavino and I were sitting in the employees' cafeteria in the
basement of the administration building.

I had chosen not to tell him about the fate of Chuy Sanchez
and his henchman. Better he not connect me to them.

"You're sure you want to do this?" he asked between bites of
a peanut butter sandwich.

"Positive."

"Even though I think it's nuts."

"Despite it."

"This took a bit of doing, you know."

"I do know."

"It's highly suspect."

"She's a kid, Paulie. Everything she extorted was returned. At the end of the day, no one lost anything. She deserves this."

"She's bound to be a repeat offender."

"Try not to be so cynical."

"Years of practice."

I grinned. "Let's go do it."

"Yeah. Okay."

We stood and headed out. "Despite your cynicism, I appreciate this, Paulie. Is there anything I can do to show my gratitude?"

"Yeah. Don't call me anymore."

She was processed out and placed in the passenger seat of my Wrangler. Her ankles were shackled and her hands cuffed. Although she appeared tired and agitated, she still exuded elegance and grace. But she regarded me with unabashed loathing.

"This isn't what you think," I told her as we waited in line at the main gate. DeSavino's Plymouth was in front of us. He was in a rapt discussion with one of the guards, presumably paving the way for our exit.

The guard waved us forward. He peered into the Wrangler.

"Catalina Sanchez?" he asked her.

"Yes."

"Buddy Steel?" he asked me.

"Yes."

After several deliberative moments, he waved us through.

I pulled up alongside DeSavino and waved. He nodded and drove away.

Catalina looked at me. "What's happening here?"

"You're free."

"What do you mean?"

"Just that. It's over. Your slate is clean."

"What are you talking about? Where are you taking me?"

After leaving the detention center, I made my way to I-5 and headed north.

"How old are you, Catalina?"

"Twenty-two. And that's not my name."

"Catalina Sanchez?"

"Catalina Sanchez is my web handle. I'm Lina. And not Sanchez. I use my mother's maiden name."

"Which is?"

She looked at me and shook her head.

"Just as well I don't know."

"I'm getting really frightened here."

"Don't. I'll take you wherever you want to go."

"What about these restraints?"

"Oh, yeah. Sorry about that."

"What sorry? Cut me loose."

"I will. But first I want to get a few things straight between us."

"Such as?"

"This is your chance for a do-over. A new start. You're free. You've had some rotten influences in your life. Your father being prime. And you've seriously misbehaved. So now you have the opportunity to either straighten up and make a life for yourself or continue down the path to self-destruction. Your call."

"Why?"

"Why what?"

"Why are you doing this?"

"Because I believe in second chances."

"And?"

"You're twenty-two years old. You displayed some technological ingenuity. Admittedly, in the service of wrongheadedness. And despite yourself, the only person truly damaged by your actions was you."

I reached into my pocket and tossed her the keys. "Now you can unshackle."

She looked puzzled for several moments. Then she undid her restraints.

"Please don't try to jump out of the vehicle. It's all okay. I promise."

"Where are we going?"

"Where do you want to go?"

"What do you mean?"

"I'll take you wherever you want to go."

"Really? Would you take me to Riverside?"

"If that's what you want. What's in Riverside?"

"My grandmother."

"Your father's mother?"

"My mother's."

"Dangerous?"

"The opposite. She hates my father."

"And you?"

"Do I hate my father?"

"Yes."

"Truth?"

"Yes."

"I might. When I was in jail, I thought a lot about him. And me. He was always so elusive. Secretive. Withdrawn. I realized I had spent my entire life trying to get his attention. Unsuccessfully, as it turns out. Chasing futility, if you get my drift."

"And your grandmother?"

"Me, she loves. She'd do anything to help me turn myself around."

A quiet came over us. As was the case with Agent DeSavino, I chose not to say anything about the fate of her father. She'd find out soon enough.

Her grandmother lived in a small tract house on a well-manicured street in a modest residential section of Riverside.

"Good luck," I said to her as I pulled up in front of the house.

"You mean I can just get out? *Adios*, goodbye?"

"You're a smart person, Lina. Take your time. Weigh your options. Make the right decision."

I took an envelope from my pocket and handed it to her.

"What's this?"

"A little assistance. You actually made some money when the value of the bitcoins skyrocketed. So here's a few bucks to help tide you over."

She opened the envelope and fanned through the bills. "This is like twenty thousand dollars or something. I don't believe this."

Her eyes narrowed and suspicion entered them. "What do you want from me?"

"I want you to take advantage of this moment. I want you to make a life for yourself."

"And that's it?"

"That's it."

She stared at me for a while. Then her eyes softened. She leaned over and gave me the briefest kiss on my cheek.

She smiled. "I don't understand why you're doing this. But I'm grateful. I won't let you down."

"Don't let yourself down."

She ran to the house and rang the bell. The door was opened by an elderly woman who stood staring at her.

Then realization dawned, and she grabbed hold of the girl and embraced her.

The girl looked back at me. She raised her hand and waved.

Then the two of them went inside, and I headed home.

FIFTY

"Here's one I'm sure you'll enjoy," Marsha Russo exclaimed when I picked up her call. "This just in. Foothills of Montecito. Summer home of Fred and Sophie Winslow. Break-in. Double homicide."

"Go on," I said.

"Protocols the same. Frozen security wires. Crooks were in the process of ransacking the place when the Winslows unexpectedly showed up."

"And?"

"When the alarm finally sounded, security found both Winslows shot to death. A great deal of blood."

"The Winslows?"

"That's just it. The Winslows died instantly. Not a whole lot of blood."

"So?"

"There was a kitchen knife beside Fred Winslow's body. The Montecito cops believe Mr. Winslow managed to wound one of the thieves with it."

"So, let me get this straight. Two invaders. Unexpectedly discovered by the homeowners. Invaders shoot the homeowners. But not before a scuffle occurs wherein one of the invaders gets knifed."

"Correct."

"So after the knifing, they manage to shoot and kill the homeowners. Then they flee the scene."

"Seems that way."

"Montecito?"

"Yes."

"Very near Santa Barbara."

"Ten miles give or take."

"J. R. McDonough."

"Excuse me?"

"Jill's father."

"What about him?"

"How can we locate his personal physician? His insurance carrier? Where he might go in a health emergency?"

"I can find that out."

"Do it."

"Because?"

"If the invaders are who we think they are, and one of them was wounded, due to their proximity to Santa Barbara, I'm surmising they'd seek treatment with someone they know. And fast."

"You want to go to Santa Barbara?"

"That's just what I want to do."

"And you want me to find out where they might have gone for help?"

"Exactly."

The call came in as I was approaching the Santa Barbara city limits.

"Doctors Murray and Larry Pruitt. Brothers. The Pruitt Clinic. High-end. Upper-class. Concierge medical service."

"Where?"

She told me.

"Sheriff Witham?"

"What about him?"

"Ask him to meet me there. I'm fifteen minutes out."

"Done."

I had known Brian Witham for some time. A career law enforcement officer, he was serving his second term as Sheriff. A no-nonsense guy in his sixties, he was sitting in his cruiser in the Pruitt Clinic parking lot when I pulled in next to him.

I briefed him as to the identities of Jeffrey Brice and Jill Nelson McDonough.

"I know the old man," Witham said. "J. R. McDonough. Crusty guy. Loaded. Wife died years ago. Always had issues with the daughter. Jill, right?"

"Right."

"Shall we?" he asked.

"You go first. The Pruitts know you. I'll cover the back."

Witham was buzzed in the front door.

I was admitted at the back door by an elderly nurse who appeared to understand why I was there.

"Jill McDonough?" she asked.

"She's here?"

"Just out of surgery."

"Jeff?"

"You mean the guy with her?"

"Yes."

"He left."

The nurse escorted me to the recovery area, where I found Brian Witham in conversation with a middle-aged doctor wearing surgical scrubs. Witham introduced me to Murray Pruitt.

"Pretty severe knife wound," Pruitt said to us. "She's lucky she survived. That should teach her to be more careful."

"Excuse me?"

"She told me she had sliced an artery while she was carving a chunk of raw steak."

I looked at Brian Witham who said, "That's what she told you?"

"She and her guy. Jeff."

"She was stabbed during a home invasion by one of the homeowners who, along with his wife, were shot and killed by Jill and her guy, Jeff."

"Oh, my God," Dr. Pruitt said. "Surely that's not true."

"Trust me," Witham said. "It's true."

"Where is Jeff now?" I asked.

"Gone to pick up some of Jill's belongings. At J.R.'s house."

"What kind of shape is she in?"

"Jill?"

"Yes."

"Let's just say she won't be up and about for a while."

"I'm going to post a deputy here, Murray. Officially, she's under arrest. She's not to go anywhere."

"Oh, my God," Dr. Pruitt said again.

Witham looked at me. "Let's take my cruiser. Get us there faster."

It took no more than ten minutes with Brian's siren blasting to reach Jill's neighborhood. We navigated the last couple of blocks in silence. I remembered the house from my earlier encounter there with her. A black Porsche 718 Spyder was in the driveway.

We parked two houses away. Both of us press-checked our weapons and headed out, Brian to the house, me hanging back in the yard, partially hidden by a live oak tree.

Brian rang the bell, which, at first, went unanswered.

Then he studied the massive picture window located on the left side of the house, adjacent to the door.

The shot fired from inside shattered the oversized window and struck him, swiveling him around, sending him reeling.

Startled, I raced to where he lay, dazed and bloodied. I knelt beside him.

The front door slammed open, and Jeff Brice came barreling through it.

He glanced briefly at Witham and me. He showed us his weapon.

Not wishing to risk any further damage to Brian, I raised my hands and dropped the Glock.

Jeff sneered at me, then he jumped into the Spyder, gunned the engine, backed out of the driveway and sped off.

I grabbed my cell and punched 911. When the dispatcher answered, I explained what had just occurred and requested immediate medical aid for Brian.

He looked at me. "I guess that was a pretty stupid move," he groaned.

"Where are you hit?"

"Arm. Side. Hurts like a son of a bitch."

"EMTs are on the way."

"Jeff?"

"At large. But we'll get him. Just like we got her."

"Bonnie and Clyde?" Brian posited.

"Dumb and Dumber," I replied.

FIFTY-ONE

Sheriff Witham was soon en route to the Santa Barbara Hospital Emergency Room.

Jeffrey Brice was in the ether.

Witham's deputy was given the assignment of notifying the Winslow family's next of kin.

Jill Nelson was still in the Pruitt Clinic. Once she was well enough, she'd be officially arrested and remanded to a federal prison facility.

I hitched a ride back to the clinic, where I was greeted by Dr. Murray Pruitt. "Have you seen it?" he asked.

"Seen what?"

"You mean you haven't been watching?"

"Watching what?"

"Come with me."

Pruitt led me into his office where a small group of employees were glued to the large-screen TV mounted on the wall across from his desk.

A car chase was taking place. Several police vehicles were following the black Porsche Spyder. On Highway 101. Heading north toward San Francisco.

"Unbelievable," I exclaimed.

The TV announcer was carrying on about the chase. It seems the driver, identified as San Remo county resident Jeffrey Brice, had shot and wounded the Santa Barbara County Sheriff, then raced off at such an excessive speed that he caught the attention of the California Highway Patrol, whose officers were now keeping close tabs on him.

At the outset, as the Porsche wended its way through the afternoon street traffic to the freeway, it not only sideswiped several parked cars, but at the intersection of High Street and Laurel Avenue, it screeched to a halt. Brice jumped out, grabbed hold of a small child who was standing with her mother on the sidewalk, and with the child in tow, he jumped back into the Porsche and sped off.

Fearing for the child's safety, the CHP officers were following the Porsche at a distance and made no move to overtake it. A CHP helicopter tracked the action from above.

According to the TV announcer, a record crowd was watching the chase unfold.

A network reporter cadged an interview with the taken child's distraught mother, who tearfully pleaded for her little girl's safe return.

The California Highway Patrol Commissioner made an

on-camera appearance wherein he assured viewers that the CHP was providing nothing short of an all-out effort to ensure the safety of the child.

The driver's father, Roger Brice, the wealthy real estate developer, had been cornered by a local TV personality and had commented that whereas he had been estranged from his son, he had just spoken with him and the young man promised to surrender. The terms and conditions for which were currently being negotiated.

"Negotiated," I muttered to myself. "What could he possibly be angling for?"

I thought how odd it was that the entitled parents of Jeff and Jill had so miserably failed them, whereas Chuy Sanchez had been totally devoted to Lina.

Dr. Pruitt caught my eye. "She's awake," he stated.

I reluctantly gave up watching the chase and stepped into Jill's room.

She stared at me vacant-eyed, the meds still clouding her mind. Then I saw recognition dawn.

"It's finished, Jill. You're toast. What I can't fathom is why you would squander a life of privilege and promise for no good reason. You had the world in your hands. And now you have nothing. Your life is as good as over. And once Jeff's in custody, the same will hold true for him. And you have no one to blame for it but yourselves."

I glared at her. "Shame on you."

Then I exited the room, slamming the door behind me.

When I got back to Murray Pruitt's office, appearing on the TV were several California Highway Patrol officers and a frazzled-looking man in a rumpled suit.

They were standing in front of Saint Catherine's Cathedral, a monstrous edifice, famous for its towering twin steeples, situated in the center of a park-like expanse of verdant lawns, indigenous trees, and oddball native shrubbery.

Cardinal Umberto Hope, an American-born prince of the Catholic Church, stood among the CHP officers and the disheveled man, who turned out to be Jeffrey Brice's father, Roger.

The commentator explained that Jeff had agreed to the terms of surrender and was now only minutes away from turning himself in to Cardinal Hope.

The black Porsche inched its way toward Saint Catherine's, closely pursued by a gaggle of photographers. When it arrived, a crowd of paparazzi materialized and swarmed around it.

Jeffrey Brice got out of the car, accompanied by his quarry, the kidnapped little girl, who appeared puzzled and disoriented.

The girl was immediately swept up by her mother. A tearful reunion.

Cardinal Hope was instantly at Jeff's side.

As was Roger Brice, who then stood self-consciously by as the Cardinal embraced Jeff.

Following which, Roger Brice reached over and awkwardly shook his son's hand.

A CHP officer read Jeff his rights and then slapped a pair of handcuffs onto him.

They were about to disperse when, all of a sudden, amid the chaos, the TV cameras discovered the kidnapped girl's mother racing toward Jeff.

Before anyone could stop her, she leaped on him and angrily raked her elongated fingernails across his face, inadvertently gouging out his left eyeball in the process.

At which point the network cut to the studio-based announcer who stared wordlessly into the camera.

That's when I'd seen enough.

I'd had my fill of these two reprobates.

As well as to the worst kind of parenting.

Good riddance to despicable rubbish.

FIFTY-TWO

The days passed uneventfully, although I was still being attended to by a small contingent of bodyguards inasmuch as the fate of Chuy Sanchez was still unknown.

A week or so later, when I arrived at the office, Marsha Russo sauntered in and dropped a copy of the *L.A. Times* on my desk.

She stood there, silently staring at me.

"What?"

"Double column header. Below the fold."

I looked at her, then picked up the paper. As she had pointed out, a two-column banner screamed: CARTEL BOSS FOUND DEAD.

It went on to inform as to where the body had been found, and for how long it appeared to have been roasting in the trunk of a Prius.

Marsha told me the story continued on a later page and when I turned to it, I spotted a blurry photo of the back of my head.

The article mentioned that the police had labeled the twin killings as being gang-related. They had no suspects and were asking anyone with information to come forward.

I looked at her.

"You know anything about this?" she asked.

"Why would I?"

"I don't know. It's just that the hat seems vaguely familiar."

"What is it you're driving at, Marsha?"

"Oh. Nothing really."

"Do you recognize the guy in the photo?"

"He might bear a resemblance to somebody. I just can't put my finger on it."

"I guess we can let the troops go now."

"You mean the officers guarding your apartment building?"

"Yes."

"You think the threat has abated?"

"Dead is dead."

She stood. "So it is. I'll stand them down."

"Thank you."

"Don't mention it."

But she didn't leave. She continued to stare at me.

Finally, I said, "What?"

"One eensy weensy question."

"Go on."

"Who do you think drove the Prius?"

"I wouldn't know. Likely some gang member."

"If only we knew."

"But we don't."

She stood looking at me.

When I didn't respond, Marsha asked, "May I quote Socrates?"

I nodded.

"As the great philosopher himself once stated, '*It isn't hard to recognize bullshit when it smacks you square in the face.*'"

FIFTY-THREE

"There's this wild rumor going around," Chanho Pineda said.

We were sitting side by side on a bench in one of Freedom's pocket parks, sipping the Starbucks lattes he had brought.

"Which is?"

"Is it true you went out on a limb on behalf of Chuy's daughter?"

"Depends on what you mean by out on a limb."

"Come on, Buddy. The girl was miraculously released from ICE detention and the charges dropped. What's up with that?"

"She had been unduly influenced by her father."

"She stole millions of dollars."

"All of which were returned. The only person who suffered from her malfeasance was her."

"Why did you do it?"

"Why do you want to know?"

"There's fresh blood sitting atop Los Perros these days and there's a degree of curiosity happening."

"Tell the fresh blood to mind its own business."

"You don't want to stir this particular pot, Buddy."

"I believe in second chances."

"Why her?"

"Call it my coply intuition."

"There's no one on the scene claiming responsibility."

"For?"

"Chuy's murder."

"So?"

"It's strange."

"What is?"

"This was a significant hit. One that should have earned the perpetrator a big reward and some serious brownie points. Everyone's been waiting for that perpetrator to step up."

"So?"

"Is this something you might know about, Buddy?"

I stood. "Are we done here, Chanho?"

He stood. "I'm betting no one's ever going to claim the reward."

I shrugged. "Ask your fresh blood to donate it to a fund for the rehabilitation of former gang members."

"Gee. What a great idea. I wish I'd thought of it."

FIFTY-FOUR

The door was opened by the Sheriff himself. He was in uniform and exuded an air of well-being. One I hadn't seen in quite some time.

"What brings you?" he asked as he ushered me into his den.

"A gift."

"What gift?"

I handed him the package I had haphazardly wrapped in plain brown paper.

He looked at it for a moment. "So chic-looking. I'm already afraid to open it."

I smiled.

It was rare indeed for us to exchange gifts of any kind. Our respective tastes rarely, if ever, coalesced. More often than not, the giver would wind up standing sheepishly in front of the givee, both of whom regarded gifts as toxic.

Burton self-consciously tore open the package, already rehearsing in his mind what he could say about it that wouldn't offend.

But when he finally got it open, he looked at it, then at me, and I spotted a tear in the corner of his eye.

Among the items the home invaders had stolen was a silver-framed color photo of the nine- or ten-year-old me standing between my parents. We were all laughing and I remember that it was my grandfather who snapped the photo—at the exact moment my Uncle Howard unexpectedly dropped his pants.

It was not only my uncle's favorite picture, but my father's as well. The one loss he truly suffered from the break-in.

He frequently lamented it, and although it took some effort, I persuaded my cousin Richard to scour the trove of photos his father had left behind in search of a copy. Which he miraculously found, scanned, and sent.

I had it framed in a sterling silver duplicate of the original and the look in my father's eye let me know I hit pay dirt.

"How did you come up with this?" he exclaimed, beaming.

"I'm happy you like it."

"Like it? I love it. It's the best picture the three of us ever took. I kept the original here. On the mantle. I looked at it every day."

We stood together, both of us engaged in a reverie of a joyful moment long past.

The old man squeezed my arm and tenderly smiled. "Thank you, Buddy. You can't know how much this means to me."

I was taken aback by his uncharacteristic show of emotion.

Particularly because it related to me and my mother and the three of us together.

When I found myself fighting back tears, I rushed to change the subject. "You look like you're dressed for bear."

"I thought I'd mosey over to the office."

"Because?"

"I don't know, Buddy. I'm feeling pretty good these days. This med cocktail has lifted my spirits."

"And you feel like working?"

"To tell you the truth, I was getting a little bored just sitting around with nothing to do. So, yes. I do feel like it. Doing what I was elected to do."

"It's good to be King."

"It is, isn't it?"

FIFTY-FIVE

Jordyn Yates and I spent the morning in the company of Mary Morigaki, a local Realtor who immediately understood what we were about and guided us to a one-bedroom apartment in a four-unit dwelling situated on a quiet, dead-end street.

We had settled on Oxnard primarily because it was halfway between Freedom and Hollywood.

The surprise was how colorful and welcoming it was, a seaside community without the hubbub of the bigger and better-known coastal cities, one that offered the same recreational and lifestyle amenities.

The apartment was steps away from a tiny private cove with a plush sandy beach.

Our plan was to use it primarily as a weekend getaway, a chance for us to test our relationship on neutral ground, in an unknown yet oddly familiar environment.

Mary had pointed out Oxnard's varied topography that offered a menu of leisurely diversions. Beaches, mountains, and flatlands, coupled with a vast array of dining and shopping opportunities offering the quintessential Southern California experience without the annoying influx of tourists.

Although the apartment was slightly costlier than we had hoped, we were smitten and signed the lease that very day.

"You won't regret it," Mary had said when we handed her the check for the rent and security. "You're going to love it here."

We both agreed we didn't want to overdo it with furniture and accoutrements. Ikea and Walmart. We made tracks for them without hesitation.

Ikea provided us with a bed and the required bedding, as well as with our basic living and dining room needs. Walmart completed the picture with kitchen and electronic apparatuses.

We had compatibly settled on all of our purchases and were in the throes of selecting a coffee maker when we experienced our first disagreement.

"You're nuts," she pronounced when I scoffed at her choice of an outrageously priced single-cup coffee maker.

"Unquestionably, it has to be a Mr. Coffee," I countered.

"A Mr. Coffee? You're kidding."

"Mr. Coffee is a whole lot better than that overpriced gas guzzler you've chosen."

"You know what, you're a total Luddite," she exclaimed, clutching the single-cup box tightly to her chest. "Wake up, Buddy. This is the coffee maker of the future."

"Not my future," I said, brandishing the Mr. Coffee package.

"Then I'll buy it myself."

"And I'll buy the Mr. Coffee myself."

"Good for you."

"Good for *you,* too! "

She stood staring at me for several moments. Then she started laughing. Hysterical, explosive, convulsive laughter.

And in no time I was laughing with her.

Customers avoided us as we continually failed in our attempts to sober up.

She put down the box and stepped over to me, threw her arms around my neck, and kissed me hard on the lips.

She leaned back and looked me in the eye. "This is the most fun I've had in years," she grinned.

"Me, too," I grinned back.

She pressed herself against me and whispered, "I love you, Buddy Steel."

Unhesitatingly, I responded, "I love you, Jordyn Yates."

We stood that way for some time.

Acknowledgments

It takes a village to bring a novel to fruition. Thus, a shout-out to all the villagers who contributed so generously to *Risk Factor*.

My gratitude to the indefatigable team at Poisoned Pen Press, led by the peerless Robert Rosenwald.

Thanks to Diane DiBiase and Beth Deveny.

And to the inimitable Michael Barson.

I'm blessed to work with Annette Rogers. *Risk Factor* is so much better as a result of her editorial prowess.

And I'm totally in debt to the amazing Barbara Peters, whose knowledge, insights, and bountiful contributions raise the bar and heighten the standards.

Thanks also to my new friends at Sourcebooks, most notably Dominique Raccah and Anna Michels.

My gratitude to the team of advance readers who always manage to spot that which I don't: Steven Brandman, Miles

Brandman, Roy Gnan, David Chapman, Thor Henrickson, and Melanie Mintz.

My thanks for the support of my longtime friend and partner, Tom Selleck.

And kudos to Tom Distler, for his encouragement and rock-solid counsel.

Plus my profound love for my late brother, Jeffrey, and for our departed parents, Selma and Arthur Brandman.

Thank you one and all.

About the Author

Michael Brandman is the author of three Jesse Stone novels, each based on characters created by Robert B. Parker, all on the *New York Times* bestseller list.

With his longtime business partner, Tom Selleck, he produced and cowrote nine Jesse Stone movies and three Westerns.

Photo by Joanna Miles

His and Emanuel Azenberg's production of Tom Stoppard's *Rosencrantz & Guildenstern Are Dead* won the Venice Film Festival's Golden Lion Award for Best Picture.

He has produced more than forty motion pictures, including films written by Arthur Miller, Stephen Sondheim, Neil Simon, David Mamet, Horton Foote, Wendy Wasserstein, David Hare, and Athol Fugard.

He is the father of two sons and lives in Los Angeles with his wife, the award-winning actress Joanna Miles.